LOVE & SINS

A LOVE & RUIN SERIES PREQUEL

J.A. OWENBY

Help! 911! My phone vibrated with a text, buzzing against the controls of the recording studio console. Seconds later, it rang, and Mackenzie Worthington's name flashed across the screen.

My pulse kicked up. It wasn't like Mac to message, then call. Something was seriously off. She was strong and independent. At times her ADHD undermined her confidence, but she was one the best friends I could have in my life, and I would do anything for her.

I cast a glance over my shoulder at John Mercer and Cade Richardson, my band members. "Hang on, guys. I have to take this." I snatched my cell up and answered Mac's call.

"Hendrix! I need your help!" Mac's voice trembled, and my heartrate went into overtime. I stood on high alert, tension snaking through my muscles that were already knotted from too many hours of writing and singing. Mac didn't make shit up or have a meltdown unless it was warranted. I could count on three fingers the number of times a frantic call had come in from her.

"Mac, calm down. What's wrong?" My attention darted around the college studio where my band, August Clover, recorded. I located my keys and black leather wallet near the equalizer controls, then stuffed my billfold in the back pocket of my jeans.

"It's Eva. She's been roofied ... I think. She's unconscious, and I can't move her on my own." Mac hiccupped through her tears.

The walls of the small room closed in on me, stifling the air I was trying to suck in. "Where are you?" I threaded my fingers through my shoulder-length hair, anticipating her response.

"A frat party ... at the Pi Kappa house."

I clenched my jaw. "Dammit, Mac. I told you and Eva those parties weren't safe." I looked at John, whose forehead was creased with worry lines. He shoved his hands into his pockets while he waited to see what was happening.

"I know, but it's too late. Please."

I could almost imagine Mac holding her breath and twirling a braided pigtail in her slender hand. "I'm on my way. Where are you? Downstairs or up?"

"We're upstairs in one of the bedrooms, and Eva is passed out on the bed. I think it's the last one on the left." She blew out a heavy sigh.

"Lock the door. Don't let anyone in until I get there. Got it?" As mad as I was that the girls were there, I had a sinking feeling that the situation was worse than what Mac was telling me so far. "I'll call you back when I'm almost there."

"Okay. Thank you. Please hurry." Mac's voice trembled, and worry wrapped its frigid talons around my chest. Eva had to be all right. She and Mac had been best friends for years, and it would tear Mac up if she weren't. Although I tried to talk myself out of the worst, I was pretty sure Mac had painted enough of a picture for me to suspect what had happened. I disconnected the call. "I have to get Mac and Eva from a frat party."

John, the drummer for August Clover, and Cade, our lead guitarist, stared at me, waiting impatiently for me to tell them what the hell was going on. The three of us along with Mac had been friends since middle school, and in high school, we started the band. One thing I'd learned over the years was that family wasn't blood related. It was made of the people I'd stitched into my heart. The ones that had been there during dark days and believed in me when I couldn't.

"Eva's in trouble. I have to hurry." I checked one last time to make sure I had all of my belongings.

John arched a blonde brow at me. "Do you need help?" He folded his arms across his chest as his light brown eyes narrowed. The guys were as protective of Eva and Mac as I was. Hell, I was pretty sure John was waiting for Eva to be legal before he asked her out. He only had to wait three more days. Eva's parents were strict and wouldn't allow her to date a college guy until she was eighteen. It didn't seem to matter that we'd all been friends for years. Shit, if I had a daughter as gorgeous as Eva, I'm not sure I'd want her dating an older guy either.

"Yeah, help would be great, but I think you need to sit this one out, John. It sounds like something might have happened to Eva. I'll keep you posted as soon as Mac tells me more."

John's face fell, fear flashing in his expression.

Cade, John, and I had been to some of these frat parties, so we understood how fast a situation could escalate. I patted his back as I headed out.

"I'll come with you." Cade hurried after me. "Is Mac okay?"

My gut squeezed tight, and I was about to vomit the pizza I'd eaten earlier in the day. "I think so, but I don't have all the details yet."

"I'll lock up," John called after us as we left the room and hightailed it down the quiet hallway. We liked to record after regular class hours since fewer people wanted those times. There were only two studios located on campus, so it was a hot commodity.

My tennis shoes smacked the pavement as I ran down the well-lit sidewalk and to the parking lot. The cool spring air carried the scent of fresh-cut grass and I stifled a sneeze.

A beep beep sounded as I pushed the button on the key fob and hurried to my new maroon Toyota Camry Dad had recently bought me. I flung the door open and climbed in as Cade hopped in the passenger's side. I started the engine.

"Dude, you know who lives at that frat house, right?" Cade stared out the window as I backed up, then shifted into drive and peeled out of the parking lot. If I didn't cool it, college security would pull me over.

"Why do you think I'm hauling ass?"

A heavy silence filled the car as I flipped on my turn signal and headed down the road. It was only a few minutes' drive away from the main campus, but it only took a few minutes to … I shoved the dark thoughts in a hole, hoping like hell nothing had happened to Eva.

"Shit. I should have known." I leaned forward, searching for a parking space within a few blocks of the party, but not finding one. "I'm getting out. Try to find a spot to park, then call me when you're on the way in, and I'll let you know where we're at." I didn't wait for Cade to respond. I was out of the car and sprinting up the sidewalk toward the sound of the music, my arms pumping as hard as they could, my hair flying behind me.

Once I arrived, I had to slow down, or I'd step on people passed out or laying on the lawn in a drunken stupor. Several kegs were near the front porch. Since there was no one around them, I assumed they were empty. With a feeling of dread in my chest, I took the stairs two at a time, then entered the crowded living room. Rhythmic beats reverberated through the speakers while boisterous laughter and raucous chatter filled the cramped space. The floor shook beneath my feet, and I attempted to slip through the drunk and sweaty bodies gyrating to "Love You Need You" by Jeffrey James.

Before I made it to the staircase, I heard my name over the song.

"It's Hendrix Harrington!" A group of girls pointed at me, then jumped up and down and started screaming.

Dammit. Even though August Clover wasn't famous, we were climbing in popularity fast. Our freshman CD had been released eight months ago, and we were booking gigs faster than we could manage them. It was quickly becoming an obsolete luxury to be out in public without being recognized. At least in Washington State.

A brunette with huge tits bounced over to me, spilling her beer on the floor as she approached. "Hi!"

"Hey, Cassie." I inwardly groaned. I didn't have time for her right now.

Cassie's hand landed on my chest and I glanced down at her, then back to my destination.

"We should get out of here," she slurred. Her fingers slid down to my crotch, and she squeezed my limp dick. I really wasn't in the mood.

I firmly grabbed her wrist. "Cassie, you're drunk, so that's a big no."

Her plump lower lip jutted out, and my focus landed on her tits. Getting laid would be nice, but not like this. Cassie had also attended high school with me, but since August Clover had grown more popular, she was bound and determined to fuck me. I wasn't entirely opposed, but my logic continued to win over my hormones. The last thing I needed was to get involved with a needy girl, and Cassie was definitely that girl.

I figured the best way to reach Mac was to give Cassie a little of what she wanted. I gently tilted her chin up with my fingers. "How about we talk about going out when you're not drunk."

She sucked on her bottom lip, and my cock suddenly woke up. "Right now, I have to find Mac."

Those were the magic words. I'm not sure why I hadn't thought about saying them to begin with. Cassie stomped her foot. "What is it with you and Mac all the time?" Cassie seemed to have forgotten she was holding her drink and folded her arms over her ample chest. The amber-colored beer sloshed over the rim of her red Solo cup and directly into her face. If I weren't desperately trying to get to Mac and Eva, I would have excused myself and laughed my ass off.

I took the opportunity to dodge her and ran up the stairs. Quickly counting the white doors, I located where I thought the girls would be. I twisted the knob, but it was locked. Relieved Mac had listened to my instructions, I raised my hand to knock, then I hesitated. I didn't want to startle her.

"Mac? Are you in there? It's Hendrix." Before I had a chance to step back, the door flung open, and a hand darted toward me. Petite fingers wrapped around my wrist, then jerked me into the room.

2

"*H*endrix!" Mac threw her arms around me. "Oh my God! You're here! Thank you so much!"

I hugged her, my gaze landing on the limp form sprawled out on the twin bed. Eva's denim miniskirt barely covered the top of her thighs, and her T-shirt was draped over her chest. At least Mac had tried, but I was still seeing Eva partly naked. "Shit." I ran a hand through my hair. "What happened?" I asked softly. From one look at Eva, I had a sinking feeling I knew what Mac was about to tell me.

"I tried to get her dressed before you got here, but I'm not strong enough to hold her up and put her shirt back on." Mac wiped her tearstained cheek. "Can we just get her out of here, then I'll fill you in?"

My phone vibrated, and I took it out of my back pocket. Cade's name popped up on my screen. I answered the call. "We're upstairs. The last door on the left." I hung up. "Cade's on his way. We only have a few minutes before he's here to help, so let's get her dressed."

I approached the side of the bed and gently propped Eva up, then I slipped behind her and held her up from the back, attempting not to see her breasts. She would be mortified if she knew, not to mention she was seventeen, and I had no business seeing her like this. Mac and I struggled but finally managed to get Eva's shirt over her head. Once her arms were through the sleeves, and her top was pulled down, I carefully laid her down again. "I'll stuff her bra and panties in my pocket. At least she has a shirt on again."

Fuck. I hadn't realized she'd had nothing on beneath her skirt. This situation was exactly what I'd thought.

A loud knock drew my attention away from the limp and sleeping Eva. "I'll get it. It should be Cade, but I'm not taking any chances." I walked across the room quickly and cracked it open.

"Good, you're here. Will you take Mac and make sure she gets to the car safely?" I asked.

"You bet." Cade's amber eyes filled with anger. "Hey, Mac. Are you all right?" His gaze landed on her and he looked Mac up and down. I assumed he was searching for any evidence she'd been hurt. The air dripped with tension as he soaked in the situation before him.

"I'm okay. We should hurry and get Eva out of here, though." Fear twisted Mac's features. "Hendrix, she can't go home. I don't know what to do." Her pitch climbed a notch.

I pressed my lips together as I realized I would have to make a call. One that I dreaded. "Mac, she has to go to the hospital. We have no idea why she's unconscious or how much she was hurt. I'll help with talking to her parents."

"Why in the hell are you here without Asher?" Cade asked, his voice teetering on unfriendly.

"We broke up, and I don't need a lecture from you right now, Cade Richardson." Mac placed her hands on her hips, clearly agitated.

"You're right." Cade tossed his hands up in surrender. "Let's go." Without another word, he crossed the room and slipped his arm around Mac's shoulders. His six-one frame dwarfed hers, which was only five-four.

"I'll carry Eva. Maybe you guys can clear a path for us." I leaned over her and scooped her into my arms. Her head lolled to the side and her nose nestled into my armpit. "Sorry about that, Eva."

"Ready?" Cade asked.

"Let's go."

Ten minutes later, I sucked in the fresh air. Spring had arrived and the sweet scent of blooming roses and daffodils lingered in the breeze.

"Oh God, I had no idea how bad it smelled in there." Mac waved a hand in front of her face as she inhaled deeply.

"Sweat, sex, stale beer, and drugs," Cade said as he led us to the sidewalk. He tossed a look over his shoulder at me. "How are you holding up, man? Even a state boxing champ has got to be wearing out a little."

Although I no longer competed, I boxed several times a week and kept in shape. "Take Mac to the car and come get me. Make it quick." Eva probably only weighed ninety pounds soaking wet, but my arms had started to burn like a motherfucker. I spotted a white brick wall and sat down. I cradled Eva protectively while I scanned the area. The party had spilled over from the house to the lawn and into the street. I was shocked the cops hadn't been called yet.

Cade knelt on the ground in front of Mac. "Hop on, shorty. A piggyback ride will be faster." Mac released a nervous giggle, then climbed on Cade's back. Even though she and Asher had dated throughout high school, I suspected she had a little crush on Cade. As long as he never took advantage of her, I wouldn't have to beat his ass. We had a good thing going with our small group, but Cade was a total whore. He could play with someone else's emotions, but not Mac's.

Eva moaned softly, and I wondered how long she would be unconscious. Mac thought she'd been roofied, but I wasn't sure how she knew that information. Maybe she was guessing from the state Eva was in.

A few minutes later, Cade arrived in my Camry. Mac hopped out of the front passenger side and opened the back door for me. "Go to the other side, Mac." I leaned into the car as far as possible with Eva still passed out, then gently placed her down. Mac knelt on the seat and wrapped her arms around Eva's torso, pulling her across the smooth tan leather.

"I'll sit with her." Mac settled in next to Eva, and I closed all of the doors.

Before I joined them, I needed to make a call. Dread stirred in the pit of my stomach as a gentle breeze dried the sweat on my forehead. I tapped the screen of my phone, then held it to my ear. It rang twice before a deep voice answered.

I ground my molars together, and I swallowed my pride. This had nothing to do with me. "I need your help." I had sworn those words would never pass my lips, but there I was, making a liar out of myself.

3

"I'll meet you at the hospital and contact Eva's parents. You did the right thing by calling me, son," Franklin Harrington said into the phone.

"I doubt Eva will see it like that." I stared into the inky black sky and noticed a few stars burned brighter than the rest.

"We can talk more, but it's better that I make the call to her parents," Dad said.

There was no way in hell I was planning on arguing with him. How would you even tell someone's parents you think their daughter had been violated? I climbed into the passenger seat and fastened my seatbelt while I continued my conversation.

"We're on our way to Sacred Heart. It's only twenty minutes from here so we will most likely beat you there." I disconnected the call, mentally preparing myself for the parental units to ask questions. Emotions would be flying high.

I slowly pivoted my attention to Cade and he nodded, then proceeded to drive down the street cautiously. The last thing we needed was to hit a drunken idiot in the middle of the road, but they were everywhere.

"Hendrix?" Mac's voice was so soft I barely heard her.

I glanced over my shoulder at the girls. "Yeah?"

"Do you think Eva is going to be all right?" Tears glistened in Mac's large brown eyes.

Shifting slightly in my seat, I struggled for the best words to say, but Mac and I had never lied to each other and I wasn't about to start now. "I don't know. If she was … if she was raped, then ..." My heart hammered against my chest, the thought sickening me that some douchebag would drug Eva, then take advantage of her while she was unconscious. Unfortunately, it was more common than I cared to think about. Thank God John wasn't with us and had gone home. I couldn't imagine what it would do to him if he saw Eva in this condition.

Mac stroked her long dark hair as she held Eva's head in her lap. "I'm scared I've already lost her. I'm not sure if she'll ever forgive me."

I frowned. There wasn't anything I liked about what Mac just said, but I knew all too well about the guilt that gutted you on a daily basis and slowly chipped away at your soul. "No. This wasn't your fault. Don't go there." I tugged my navy polo shirt out of anger and frustration.

"If I'd stayed with Eva nothing would have happened to her." Mac chewed her bottom lip and watched out the window as the neighborhoods passed by.

"That's not true. If she was in fact roofied, even if you were with her, the second you looked away someone could have slipped something into her drink. Hell, you could have been drugged too."

"But I would have seen when she started acting weird. Instead, we gravitated toward two different guys, then she was gone." Mac shook her head, shame washing over her face.

"Eva makes her own choices, Mac. You both do. The only reason she would blame you is because she'll be angry and scared at first, not because she really thinks it's your fault."

"Mac, any guy that drugs and rapes a girl is a piece of fucking shit. *He* is to blame. Not you and not Eva. And if you need me to remind you of that later, I will." Cade grew silent and he clenched the steering wheel until his fingers were white.

Cade was right but what sucked was that some people would say Eva had no business drinking at the frat party at only seventeen. I couldn't disagree with that logic. I told them not to go, but Eva wasn't to blame. Even if she'd ran through the house naked, no one had a right to touch her. Not one fucking person.

Cade pulled into the hospital emergency area, and I hopped out before the car had stopped entirely. I flung open the door, scooped Eva into my arms, and hurried to the entrance. Mac was right behind me.

The next few minutes were a flurry as the nurses whisked Eva away on a gurney, and Mac provided as much information as she had to the front desk.

"Her parents should be here soon." I glanced down at Mac, who had wrapped her arms around her waist, her fingers clenching and unclenching into a fist. Taking one of them in mine, I gave her a gentle squeeze. When Mac was stressed, two things happened: her ADHD escalated, and she ate. A lot. As in she could eat more than Cade and I combined.

"Let's have a seat and wait for Eva's parents and Cade." I continued to hold her hand as we settled into a few chairs against the wall. The emergency room was calmer than I assumed it might be, but it was almost eleven on a Friday night.

"I can't sit right now." Mac wiped her palms along the thighs of her skinny jeans, then she began to pace across the white tile floors.

"Have you and Asher talked lately?" I sank into the blue hard plastic chair. My hope was to distract her from thinking about Eva, but I wasn't sure if it would work or not.

"No. I'm pretty sure we're really over. As in no longer together. Finished. Caput. Like, how did we get here? Don't answer that. I already know, but sometimes it hurts so fucking bad I have to lie to myself about what happened. We were talking about getting engaged after graduation, then ..." Grief and sadness flickered across her face. She massaged her forehead with the palm of her hand

and continued wearing a path in the tiled hospital floor.

Before I could respond, the front doors whooshed open, and a rush of chilly air preceded Cade. Even though it was April, the night temperature in Spokane still dropped to the thirties.

"Any word about Eva yet?" Cade sidestepped Mac and sank into the chair next to me.

"No," Mac replied.

"Hendrix," a deep voice called from the entrance.

My head snapped up, and I stood while the steel walls I'd built around my heart automatically slammed into place.

Mac's mouth gaped, then she closed it and shot me a glare. Her following words came out in a hiss. "Why is *he* here?"

4

"To protect you." I hadn't told Mac I'd called my dad. It wasn't as though I wanted him here either, but we needed his attorney skills.

"Mac, are you all right?" Dad asked, assessing her. Before she could answer, he pulled her into a tight hug.

"Yeah … no." She slowly slid her arms around his waist.

Jessica, the last girl I'd dated, had said Dad and I were nearly mirror images of each other. I disagreed. He was taller and leaner than I was. He cleared me by a couple of inches, and I was thicker in the chest and arms. However, we had the same piercing blue eyes and brown hair. Mine almost reached my shoulders, and Dad had consistently kept his short. He always dressed for business, including that night. We were opposites in that department. While he wore black dress slacks with a blue button-down Stefano Ricco shirt and black Berluti loafers, I lived in jeans and T-shirts or polo shirts.

Mac stepped back and her attention darted over to Cade and me.

"Tell me what happened, Mac." Dad gently squeezed her shoulder.

"I ..." She sucked in a deep breath. "Okay, so ... Hendrix told me to stay away from the frat party, but Eva was bound and determined to go. I told her it was a bad idea, but she had already made up her mind to go with or without me, so I gave in. I couldn't let her go alone ..." Mac scrubbed her face with her hands, then dropped them by her sides and began pacing in front of us again. "We had a few drinks. Just beer, you know? I thought it would be safer ... I got a little tipsy, but nothing serious. Eva was a few feet away chatting with some guy and this other dude came up to me and we started ... uh ... talking and stuff. Before I knew it, half an hour had passed. I searched the crowd for Eva, but I couldn't find her, and I freaked out."

Dad folded his arms across his chest, a sign that he was processing. His lawyer mind was fully engaged at this point. "Was that normal for her, Mac?"

"Sometimes." Mac hedged. She shook her head, tears welling in her eyes. "Yeah. She was notorious for having a few drinks then disappearing with a guy or two. I had stopped going to parties with her because I felt more like a babysitter than being able to hang and have fun. I mean, do I look like a babysitter? Do you know why I didn't want to watch her every move? Because if something awful happened it wouldn't be my fault. But tonight, I knew better. Franklin, I screwed up," Mac gushed. She nervously toyed with the hem of her red shirt.

I stood and slid my arm around Mac's shoulders. "It's not your fault. Eva makes her own decisions. Everyone makes mistakes, Mac."

"Hendrix is right. You can't keep up with her all the time. Eva knows what can happen at these parties," Cade added.

Mac narrowed her gaze at him and she placed her hands on her hips. Cade tossed his hands up in surrender before Mac let him have it. "I didn't mean it like that. Honest. It's been a stressful night."

Mac's expression softened. "I know. I'm just edgy."

Dad sat down and propped his ankle on the opposite knee. He appeared to be relaxed, but I knew better. He was pissed. Maybe at Mac or maybe Eva. Maybe both. I wasn't sure. I did know that he needed to be careful and not cross a line with me.

"Mac, the police will question you. I'll be with you. I want to ensure they act appropriately."

Understanding slipped over Mac's face, and she looked up at me. "That's why you called him."

I gave her a half shrug. "You know Dad taught me to cover all the bases."

Mac stood up on her tiptoes and kissed my cheek. "Thank you for coming."

My phone buzzed, and I retrieved it from my back pocket. A text from John flashed across my screen.

Is everyone okay?

My thumbs danced across the keyboard.

I'll fill you in soon. We're at the hospital, and Eva has been admitted. We're waiting for her parents to show up.

Dad cleared his throat. "We should get on the same page before the cops arrive. I need to know exactly what you saw."

Mac gulped and removed my arm before she slowly began pacing back and forth again. "As soon as I realized she wasn't in the living room or kitchen, I hightailed my ass upstairs. I knocked on every door and flung open the ones that weren't locked. I pissed off a few people." She barked out a nervous laugh. "Anyway, I finally reached the last room and barged in." Her cheeks paled and she wrung her hands. "Eva was mostly naked, and a guy was on top of her." Mac's voice hitched with her last words. "It took me a minute to realize what I was seeing. Eva wasn't moving at all, but he was. He was having sex with her. Like I *saw* it." She slammed her eyes closed briefly. "Hendrix, Cade, and John have always told me to grab anything close by if I were in a bad situation. I spotted a hockey stick and whacked him on the back."

I couldn't help the huge grin that spread across my face. "Good job."

"At least it stopped him. I honestly think he was so absorbed with what he was doing to Eva he didn't hear me walk into the room. Anyway, he hopped off the bed and jerked his jeans up. That's when he looked directly at me, and I saw who it was."

Dad shot up out of his chair. "Are you sure? Was it dark?"

"Two lamps were on. I could see fine," Mac assured him.

A beat of silence hung in the air.

"Who was it, Mac?" Dad asked gently.

Mac gave me a sideways glance, and I nodded for her to continue. I was pretty sure I already knew who it was, but she hadn't verbalized it yet.

"Brandon Montgomery," Mac whispered, fear evident in her expression.

"That motherfucker!" Cade's nostrils flared as he ran a hand through his dark hair.

Dad didn't even miss a beat after Cade's outburst. It wasn't as though he hadn't heard us all swear before.

"This is big." Dad rubbed his fingers along his clean-shaven jawline.

"It's why I didn't want you and Eva at that party, Mac. Brandon lives there and he's a fucking bastard. I'm not sure when he changed, but he's sure as hell not the same guy I went to high school with."

Seconds later, Eva's parents and the police arrived.

"We'll talk more after we get home," Dad said to me.

"There's nothing else to say." I ground out my response, my shoulders rigid. Dad might be able to pretend everything was okay between us, but it was far from it.

Mac's mom, Janice Worthington, arrived a few minutes later. I suspected that she'd crawled out of bed and rushed over to the hospital. Her long blonde hair was piled on the top of her head in a messy bun and dark circles shadowed her brown eyes.

Janice was always working long hours as a single mom, but she never complained when all of us were over a few times a week for dinner. Feeding three college guys and Mac wasn't cheap. It's why I helped Mac keep their house clean and mowed the grass in the summer. Hell, I'd been running my dad's place since I was ten. I knew how to get shit done and well.

Once a week, I cooked for everyone at Dad's place, but Janice never came over, so I took a lot of leftovers and stocked her fridge. Maybe it was weird, but to me, that's what you did for family. Janice had opened her home and heart to me, and I swore I'd never take it for granted.

Janice embraced Mac and kissed the top of her head. "Mac, are you all right?"

Mac nodded. "Eva's not."

"Can someone fill me in?" Janice's focus landed on Dad, and the air between them crackled like an approaching storm. "Thank you for calling me, Franklin."

"Of course." Loose change jingled as Dad shoved his hands in his pockets. "I'll be with her during questioning as well."

Janice pursed her lips. "I would appreciate it. I don't know what they're allowed to ask or not. I can be with her, but you're the one with the expertise."

A sharp ache spread through me, and my chest tightened as I watched Dad and Janice's gazes lock for a moment. There had been so much damage. So much pain. I wasn't sure how we would ever move past it all.

The next few hours dragged by as the nurses and doctors confirmed that Eva had been raped. Now it was just a matter of waiting to see if Brandon had left evidence. If so, the case would be a slam dunk in court, and that sorry son of a bitch would finally get what was coming to him. At the same time, my heart splintered with the news. It was one thing to suspect something, another to hear it confirmed.

Once the police had taken the information they needed from Mac, she was free to go.

"I'll stop by tomorrow." I hugged her. "Try to get some sleep, but you know you can text if you need me."

"Me too," Cade said from behind me.

"Thanks for all your help tonight. Both of you." Mac gave us a little wave, then wrapped her arms around her tiny waist. She gave me a wistful smile as she followed Janice out of the hospital.

My phone buzzed in my back pocket, and I removed it. A text from John flashed across my screen.

The FBI is here.

5

---

*J*ohn had been living in our guesthouse for the last four months. When his piece of shit father, Randy, was arrested for espionage, John had nowhere else to go. Randy had been a sergeant in the Marines and was a drill instructor until he was caught. The second John's father was in trouble, his mom took off and never reached out to her son again. In a matter of minutes, John lost his parents and home. They'd all been close and often took long trips together, but that was over now.

Without a second thought, Dad had offered him a place to live rent-free. It was moments like those that thawed my heart a little toward Dad, but it wasn't enough to heal the damage.

John living down the hill from the main house worked well for me too. We were constantly talking music, lyrics, and the new beats John was working on. He walked around with his drumsticks in his hands and often practiced new licks on an imaginary drum or a piece of soft furniture.

He and Cade weren't my best friends. They were my brothers. They'd stuck with me during some dark days in middle school and high school and not once had they ever given me crap about mentally checking out of reality. More times than I could count, John, Mac, and I had hung out playing video games until five in the morning. Cade had to be home at night due to his family responsibilities, so he rarely joined us for an all-nighter. Even though he never verbalized it, I suspected at times John was afraid to leave me alone. He never made a big deal of it either. John just hung out and kept it low-key. I believed he was the reason I was alive. On the days I didn't think I could take any more, I reminded myself I couldn't hurt the people I loved. Somehow it was enough to hold on to until life got better.

Music had also been my sanctuary. Once the band was signed and I was consistently writing, my world righted itself again. Needless to say, I was happy that Dad and I were in a position to help John, and I was able to return the favor.

After we left the hospital, Cade grabbed an Uber and headed home while I followed Dad back to the house. I slowed my Camry as I took a sharp curve and steered along the winding driveway. My headlights landed on the four-car garage as I parked next to Dad's black Porsche.

Two men in black business suits caught my attention as they approached Dad's car, and I slowly climbed out of mine. For some reason, I thought the FBI was there for John. I'd assumed they had questions concerning his father, but that's not what this looked like … at all.

I stood quietly, hoping to overhear Dad and the men, but their hushed tones were too quiet. Dad turned to me. "Son, you should go inside."

"I'm going to talk to John." I flipped my key ring around my first finger, eyeing the men while I strolled by as though I didn't have a care in the world. If these men were talking to Dad about an old case, then I planned on keeping my distance. Besides, I didn't know shit about Dad's clients. Dad was tight-lipped when it came to his business.

Questions spun around in my head, and my mind buzzed with a million scenarios of why the FBI wanted to speak to Dad. Although he was a well-regarded and high-profile attorney, he hadn't practiced in a few years, but I had a feeling that was about to change.

I rapped my knuckles against the guesthouse door.

"Come in!" John yelled.

I walked in, then gently closed it behind me. "Dude, I thought the FBI was here about your father." I walked to the kitchen, opened the fridge, and grabbed a Heineken. The black-and-white granite countertops were stripped clean of any items except a coffee pot. John had always kept everything nice, which was cool.

"You and me both. I figured they were still investigating Randy." John laced his fingers behind his blonde head, his whiskey-colored eyes attentive.

John never referred to Randy as his father anymore, and I didn't blame him.

"I know you and Franklin have your issues, and I'm not pressing for you to give him a second chance, but at least he's here. He's finally showing up for you, man. For all of us. If it weren't for him, I'm not sure where I'd be."

"Nah, I would have smuggled you into my room." I grinned at him as I imagined shoving all six feet of him into the corner of my closet. I understood what John was saying about Dad finally being present, but a few nice favors and a new car didn't fix years of shit. Right now wasn't a good time to talk about it anyway. I redirected the conversation. "Fuck, it's been a long night." After removing the lid from the bottle, I flopped down on the black suede sofa.

I stretched my legs in front of me, my attention landing on the light-colored hardwood floors and black area rug. A flat-screen television hung over the gas-burning fireplace. There were three small bedrooms and two bathrooms. At seventeen hundred square feet, it was cozy yet spacious. Cade, John, Mac, and I hung out here all the time.

John took a long pull of his beer, then set it down on the end table. "How's Eva?" He leaned over, planting his elbows on his knees as worry lines creased his forehead.

I hesitated. John would keep his mouth closed, but it was still difficult to talk about. "The doctor confirmed she was roofied and raped tonight."

The color drained from John's cheeks and his

nostrils flared. "Who? Who hurt her?" He whispered through clenched teeth.

"Mac said it was Brandon." His name left a disgusting, foul taste in my mouth.

John shot off the couch, fury rolling off him in waves. "That sick bastard. Why would she have gone to a fucking frat party where he lives?"

"I asked myself that same question." I took another drink, mulling over ways to catch Brandon alone at night and inflict a large amount of pain on him. After what he'd done to Eva, I wasn't sure I could keep my temper in check any longer. "I don't think the girls knew he lived there. I suspect they wanted to see what a frat party was like. They'll be at the college in September, so I understand their curiosity. I just wish they'd told me they were bound and determined to go. We could have gone with them."

"Do you think Eva will remember anything?" He placed his hands on his hips, and pain etched into his expression. "Goddammit. I was going to ask her out and spoil her for her birthday."

"Yeah, you're probably going to have to wait on that." I didn't really need to state the obvious. John was an intelligent guy, but I was wrestling for something to say. Honestly, I wasn't sure if Eva would ever recover from what happened. I had no clue. As far as I knew, I hadn't ever personally known anyone who had been assaulted before. "They did a rape kit, so if Brandon left any traces of DNA, then he'll serve time. Eva's parents are from here and well known in the community. Everyone I know loves them. I can't see this going well for Brandon if it goes to court."

"He better be charged." John sank into the couch, and the muscle in his jaw twitched as he stared ahead. "I wonder if she'll take my call if I reach out to her tomorrow?"

"I have no idea, man. You should try, though. I'll be checking on Mac tomorrow, too. I'll ask her if she's talked to Eva and keep you in the loop."

I stood slowly and finished off my beer. "I'm going to head up to the main house and see if the FBI is still around. Maybe I can find out some details."

"Good luck with that. Your dad is tight-lipped as hell."

"I know, but I've gotta try. It's not every day the FBI stops by." I told John goodnight and left. Tugging my phone out of my back pocket, I glanced at the time. It was nearly one in the morning. The day was barely beginning.

I trudged up the steep hill and shivered. The cold air crept down my neck and the back of my polo shirt while I picked up my pace. Before I realized it, a hulking figure stepped in front of me. *What the fuck?*

6

My instincts nudged me hard. What in the hell was this dude doing on our property at night? I took a few steps back, gaining some space between us as my arms automatically raised to my chest. I had no idea who this man was, but I would beat the shit out of him if he tried to hurt my family.

"You're Hendrix, aren't you?" The big guy moved out of the shadows. He easily reached six foot three, and his sharp brown eyes assessed me. He wore a dark jacket, which made it more difficult to see him since the trees were blocking the moonlight.

"Yeah. Who are you, and why are you lurking

around my house like a murderer?" My hands clenched into fists.

"I'm Franklin's new bodyguard. He sent me to find you."

Bodyguard? I held his gaze and stood my ground. "Why would he need security?"

"That's not for me to say. I'm Charles. You'll see me around consistently, so I wanted to introduce myself."

"That was a hell of an introduction, don't you think?" I slowly lowered my arms.

"I was on the way to the guesthouse." His tone was cool and bordered on unfriendly. Whoever this guy was, he was all business.

"John is there." I watched him carefully and didn't move.

Charles nodded but remained still.

"Is there something else I can help you with?" Internally, I bristled. I didn't like him. At all.

"I'll escort you." He motioned for me to proceed.

What the fuck is going on?

I took a step, then Charles fell in next to me. Without a word, we walked to the back patio together. I flung open the kitchen door as Charles followed me inside, then flipped the locks into place.

"Dad?" I called out.

"He's in his office," Charles said.

"Excellent." I hurried past the refrigerator and stove and into the formal dining room, then took a sharp left down the hall. Dad's office was next to his bedroom. They were the only two rooms in this part of the ten thousand square foot house, which allowed him the privacy he needed.

Reaching the room, I knocked, announcing my presence. Charles remained in the hallway behind me.

"Close the door, son." Dad peered up from his laptop, his tone no-nonsense. Dark shadows had settled beneath his blue eyes. It had been a long night, and it was obviously wearing on him.

I did as he asked, then sank into the black leather wingback chair. My attention landed on the pictures that lined his bookcases along with his legal books. The problem was that all of the photos were from years ago, and not a single one of them included my mother. Everyone in Dad's life had left him. I was the first one that had come back, willing to give him another chance. I'd only moved in with him again six months ago. For some reason, I'd agreed to live with him again, but some days I wasn't sure why. My mom had disappeared when I was three, so I'd stomped out any flame of hope that she would miraculously appear on the doorstep and whisk me away a long time ago.

Dad closed his computer and leaned back in his leather executive chair, pulling me away from my thoughts. Anxiety hummed beneath my skin while he steepled his fingers together and appeared deep in thought, worry lines creasing his forehead.

"Who is Charles and why is he here?" I asked in an attempt to get the conversation rolling.

"He's my bodyguard and yours when you're out. If I need to, I'll hire more, but for now, we'll see how this works."

I shifted in my seat, trying to be patient and wait for some kind of explanation.

"You saw the FBI here. I can't divulge any information, but it's best if we have some protection. Besides, August Clover is gaining popularity every day. You guys are recording another album and have performance dates scheduled. It would be smart to adjust to security accompanying you."

"We're not that big." His excuse was lame, but I wasn't making any headway with him. I assumed that would be how it played out. It's not like you can blab about what the FBI is working on.

"Are you in trouble, Dad?" That was all I really needed to know. "Did you do something you shouldn't have on a case?"

"No, it's nothing like that. I'm not under investigation. I promise."

The information should have helped my nerves settle down, but it hadn't.

I leaned forward, my gaze connecting with his. "What happens when I move out? Will you hire a bodyguard for me as well?"

Dad folded his hands on top of his desk. "I thought you were going to stay for a while." Sadness flickered across his features.

"I've saved enough money for a down payment on a house. I'd like to support myself now that the band is taking off."

A smile eased across Dad's face. "I can respect that. It's a big step and responsibility. If the water heater goes out, it's up to you to replace it. All of the maintenance is on your shoulders."

"I know. I've talked to Janice about it." I hadn't meant for that to fly out of my mouth, but I was closer to her than I was Dad.

"I see." Dad blew out a sigh and a pregnant pause filled the room. "Are we ever going to be okay, Hendrix?"

My stomach flip-flopped. I wouldn't lie to

him, but the truth didn't make me feel any better either. "I don't know."

Vulnerability washed over his face. "What can I do to set things right again?"

"Again?" I barked out a laugh. "Things between us have never been all right." I shook my head, surprised he would think they had ever been okay.

Dad stood and walked around his executive cherrywood desk.

"Hendrix ... I'll never forgive myself for what happened to Ken—"

"Don't." I held my hand up to stop him while the anger beneath my calm façade rolled to a boil, threatening to overflow if he continued. "Don't say her name. *Ever.*"

"We have to talk about it, son."

Tension sizzled between us. "Why? So you can go to an Alcoholics Anonymous meeting and say that you made amends to me? Will that help you get up in the morning and look yourself in the eye?" My hand clenched tightly and my fingernails dug into my palm, shooting pain through my arm. I took a deep breath. "You were passed out drunk when it happened. I begged you to stop drinking that day ... *every* day, but it wasn't enough. My pleading was never enough for you. *I* was never enough." The words surged out of my mouth without permission. On the awful days, I could still smell the burnt rubber … the … I quickly retreated into my head and blocked out the memories—my entire being buzzed with my churning emotions.

"That's not true. You were *always* good enough. It was me. What happened wasn't your fault, Hendrix. Please give that pain and anger back to me. It's not yours to carry." Tears welled in his eyes. "It's been a year since I've had a drink. I realize I was a lousy father and husband. Dealing with how I treated everyone back then …" He shook his head. "I'm so sorry. All I want to do is try to make it right. I have this talented, strong, smart son who I might have lost along with everyone else, and it's killing me."

His words caught me off guard. He had never apologized for his drinking before. The steel walls I'd built around my heart lowered a bit, and I sank into my chair. "You've never said you were sorry before." I choked on my words, grief seizing my throat.

"I meant every word I said, Hendrix. Those years … you carried so much. You were running this place by the time you were ten with Ruby's help. After that day—" He choked on his words. Neither of us was ready to talk about it yet.

My heart played tug-of-war with my mind. I wanted Dad to stay sober and rebuild his life. Even though I wouldn't admit it, I needed him. I needed him to be a good father and show the fuck up for a change. A little voice inside my head began pointing out all the times he had shown up over the last year. Maybe I couldn't see his efforts beyond the resentment I still clung to, but sometimes my anger protected me from being emotionally destroyed. I'd clawed my way out of the pits of despair once, and I refused to go down with him again.

"It's really been a year?" I fished around in my front pocket for a hairband, then slid it onto my wrist. My therapist had taught me that when I felt myself slipping into uncontrollable anger or dealing with flashbacks, popping the hair tie against my wrist would help bring me back to the present moment. I wasn't there yet, but I'd learned to identify the physical warnings when I was teetering on the edge. This conversation sucked, and even with the hurricane of feelings crashing down on me, I couldn't imagine how Dad felt.

"Yeah. I got my one-year chip last week." Dad

shoved his hand into the pocket of his slacks, then removed a round coin.

I rubbed my thumb along my brow line, trying to conceal my surprise. Was he really serious about changing? A seed of hope had just been planted in my heart. I instinctively wanted to snuff it out, but I couldn't. He'd never gone without a drink for an hour, much less a year.

"I carry the chip with me to remind myself that every day I have a choice, and that I made good decisions for three-hundred-and-sixty-five days in a row." Dad sat on the edge of his desk, his blue-eyed gaze remaining on me.

"Wow. I hadn't thought of it like that. That's impressive, Dad."

When I was thirteen, I'd finally confided in Mac how bad it was at home, and the next thing I knew, Janice and Mac showed up here and packed up my belongings. Janice had cleaned up the guest room at her place and moved me in. There was no discussion. Janice just took charge. It wasn't long after that I started writing music and singing. It was the creative outlet that provided me with a safe way to express all of my grief and fear. Janice and Mac had supported me every step of the way. That was what family was all about.

I toyed with the hem of my shirt. Maybe it was time I allowed Dad in a little. We could take it one day at a time and see what happened, but I needed some space to allow my heart to heal.

My attention dropped to the beige carpeted floor, then to Dad. "Do you want to help me look for a house?"

7

A huge grin broke out over Dad's face, and I found myself smiling as well. I'd forgotten what he looked like when he was happy. "I'd be honored. How can I help?"

"I need an agent. You know a lot of people ... maybe you could connect me with someone you trust?"

Dad strolled to his chair, then pulled open a drawer. "Here. Gabrielle is fantastic. We attended high school together. She's highly recommended." Dad removed a business card and handed it to me. "Give her a call. If you want to ... tell her you're my son."

"Thanks. Would you like to look at some properties with me when she has some lined up?

Maybe you can weigh in on them since you've been a homeowner since I've known you." I huffed a laugh, another grin breaking free at my joke.

"I'd love to be a part of the process. Can I ask what you'd like in a home?" Dad sank into his office chair, obviously more relaxed than he was twenty minutes ago.

"Three bedrooms. Mac will start college in a few months, so she'll have a room if she wants to hang out at my place. My first-year roomie sucked, so I want to be there for her in case she needs me."

"I think that would mean a lot to her. Do you want acreage?"

"No. Not now but maybe someday. I figure a house will be enough to take care of. I'd like a nice patio so I can entertain. Down the road, I'd like to add a recording studio, but I can't afford it yet."

"I can help." Dad was testing the water. One thing he hadn't lost during his years of being a drunk was his money. It continued to work for him even when he was passed out. Dad wasn't just rich. He was a multi-millionaire, and if I ever pushed the issue, I could have a few million dollars in my bank account, but that's not who I was.

Although Dad had paid for my car and college, I wanted to stand on my own two feet. If he could make millions, I could too.

"I appreciate it, but it's an accomplishment I have on my to-do list. Plus, I'll need to design the acoustics and space. It will be my baby, so I prefer it to be everything I want."

"In some ways, I suspect the studio will be more personal to you than the rest of the place." Dad's tone was full of understanding and respect. He leaned back in his chair, and it creaked beneath him.

"Probably. I think it will help me to look at some different types to see what I like. I'm actually excited." I rubbed my hands together, anticipating my own space to sing and write any time I chose to. I'd revel in the peace and quiet and allow the words to flow.

A beat of silence filled the space between us, and Dad scratched his chin. "I'm sorry that we need security. I don't think that will change any time soon, though."

I leaned forward. "And you promise that this isn't about you? I mean the FBI isn't accusing you of something bad?" A prickle of panic rippled over my body. "Just be honest. Please."

Dad propped his elbows on his desk, his expression filling with sincerity. "They were here to let me know we needed at least one bodyguard. I'm not under investigation, nor have I broken any laws. My business and legal license are in good standing. You have my word."

A year ago, his promises were empty and meant nothing to me or anyone else. This would be a good test to see if he was blowing sunshine up my ass or if he was really telling me the truth. My gut said to believe him, but I wanted proof. Every time he was honest and showed up for me, I knew a piece of my heart could heal again. Dad and I were making progress, but we weren't quite there yet.

"Okay." There wasn't anything left to say, but I'd definitely be watching to see how all of this played out.

"How's Mac after last night?" Dad asked.

Suddenly the tick of the clock caught my ear as each second announced itself. It was nearly two in the morning. I stifled a yawn.

"I'll check on her tomorrow, but she was a mess when she and Janice left the hospital. I wish she'd listened to me and not snuck off to the party. I mean I'm assuming Eva's parents had no idea where she was. If she'd told me Eva was hell-bent on going, Cade, John, and I would have gone with them. I would have made sure nothing happened."

"Don't take the responsibility for this situation, Hendrix. This isn't on you, so don't pick it up. You spoke with Mac, and the girls made their choice."

I rubbed my face with my hands and blew out a heavy sigh. "I'm not. All I'm saying is this didn't have to happen." I fidgeted in my seat like a little kid sitting on the front row pew in church. The reminder of Brandon's assault sent a jolt of anger through me. "Something has to be done about Brandon, though. I don't think Eva is his first."

"What do you hear around campus?" Dad's gaze was sharp and attentive as he waited for me to reply.

I rolled my shoulders, attempting to ease the tension seizing my muscles. "That he's racking up numbers. I've heard of at least five other girls he's hurt … and before you say it—" I raised a hand to stop him from interrupting. "—yeah, I know they're rumors, but I'm leaning toward believing them. Any time his name is mentioned, you can see the alarm in people's expressions. The girls are afraid of him, and the guys are too. He's a trained boxer, and I've seen him go after his opponent in the ring. He's vicious and doesn't play by the rules. I can't imagine what would happen without a ref to pull him off the other guy."

"Do you personally know anyone else other than Eva that he's hurt? The more girls that are willing to testify against him, the better," Dad explained, his forehead creasing. I detected frustration and a hint of anger in his cool tone.

A horrible thought slammed into my chest, nearly leaving me breathless. "Dammit. Mac and Eva will have to testify while that piece of shit is staring at them in the courtroom, won't they? There's no way Eva's parents will encourage her to do that. The defense attorney will tear her up. Dad, you can't let that happen." My pulse kicked into overdrive. "If Brandon learns they're testifying—that Mac is …" Fear bundled inside me, and my stomach churned. I couldn't finish my sentence.

"We have to see if there's evidence first. Try not to jump to any conclusions. I'll reach out to a few friends and see what I can do to get a rush on the results. But if there's DNA, he could be prosecuted for second-degree rape." Dad was an expert at hiding his emotions since he was an attorney, but I didn't miss his fisted hand before he moved it to his lap.

Crossing my arms over my chest, I attempted

to take Dad's advice. "I'm torn," I admitted. "I don't want Mac and Eva to have to testify against Brandon. They'll be a target. He'll make them miserable. On the other hand, it has to be stopped."

"I'm on the same page as you are, son." Dad glanced at the clock. "There's nothing that can be done tonight, though. Why don't we get some sleep?"

I rose and stretched, my knees popping loudly. "That's probably a good idea. Tonight has kicked my ass and I'm tired. I'll let you know what I learn after I see Mac tomorrow. I'll also call the realtor." I held up the business card I forgot I was holding. "Thanks for the help."

"Thank you for allowing me to." Dad walked over to me and opened the door. He patted me on the back as I left the office and entered the hall-way, where the big-ass bodyguard was waiting for us. I didn't think I'd ever get used to someone lurking around all the time.

I shrugged past Charles and made my way to the kitchen. My stomach growled as I approached the stainless steel fridge and opened it. Grabbing a Coke, I searched the refrigerator for something with some substance to it. After I moved a few items, my attention landed on a casserole dish. I set the soda on the tan marble countertop and lifted the corner of the aluminum. My mouth watered as I identified it as Ruby's lasagna. Her cooking was the best part of moving back in for a while. Plus, I was able to save up for my own place.

After I heated my food, I collected my drink and plate and headed up the stairs to my bedroom. At least I had the top floor to myself. There were three huge bedrooms with en suite baths and a game room that you could easily pack fifty people into. I just never had friends over except when I cooked dinner once a week.

I reached my room and nudged the door open with my elbow. The safety lock dangled from the latch I'd added to the frame years ago. I hadn't had to use it since I'd moved back in, which was progress. I couldn't recall how many times I'd come home from middle school and found Dad passed out in my bed in a puddle of vomit. At the time, Ruby had left as well, so I was constantly cleaning up a goddamned mess.

Waving my elbow in front of the light sensor, I approached my nightstand and sat my plate down. I tossed the extra pillows onto the other side, then tugged off my shirt and threw it onto the king-sized bed. Before I moved back in, Ruby had shopped for new sheets and a black feather comforter for me. I loved how thoughtful she was.

Exhaustion crept over me as I located the TV remote and turned on the flat-screen TV for some noise as I rifled through my dresser for a comfy pair of sweats. I never slept in my boxer briefs. Those difficult years had taught me to be ready for an emergency night or day. Living with Dad had never been boring.

After Marion, Dad's third wife, had left, I was rarely able to sleep through the night without Dad stumbling into my room or knocking on my door if I'd locked him out. One evening, he'd set off the alarm system, and I found him outside passed out in the driveway. If I hadn't slept at least partially dressed, I'm not sure what trouble he might have gotten into while I scrambled to find some clothes.

The dingy green of my stuffed turtle caught my eye from the top of my bookshelf. The seam in his belly had started to split open, and a little bit of fluff poked out. I strolled over to it and picked him up. I remembered the toy, but not the person that had given it to me. My mom. Dad said I drug it around with me everywhere I went until I was in first grade. It was the only gift I still had from Mom. Dad assured me she'd given me more, but where were they? Had he thrown them away after she'd left, and I was too young to remember?

I scolded myself for keeping it. The memories of her had faded into the darkness. I'd given up on her a long time ago, but for some reason, I couldn't talk myself into discarding my turtle.

Emotionally drained, I removed my jeans and slipped on my navy sweatpants, then flopped into bed. My stomach growled, reminding me that it had been a long ass time since I'd eaten anything. Staring blankly at the television, I ate my late-night dinner and relished in the Italian spices and cheese flavors bursting on my tongue. Finally full and more relaxed, I allowed myself to drift off to sleep where Brandon's evil sneer waited for me in my dreams.

8

————————

*B*right sunlight filtered through the cracks of my navy blackout curtains. I pulled the comforter over my head, unwilling to wake up. My mind drifted through the hazy remnants of my sleep and reminded me that I was supposed to go to Mac's today. I groaned and tossed the warm blankets off me. Staring blankly at the ceiling, I smoothed my hair off my face and sighed. My thoughts took a sharp turn to last night and Charles. Dad had a bodyguard. A fucking bodyguard.

I sat on the edge of the bed and dug my toes into the thick, plush carpet, the softness of the silk fibers tickling my feet. After a good stretch, I reached for my cell on my nightstand—no messages, which was a positive thing. Hopefully Mac got some sleep last night. I was suddenly eager to see her and Janice and ask for an update on Eva.

Tapping the Spotify app on my phone, I connected it to the speakers in the ceiling. Citizen Shade's voice filled my room as he sang "Forfeit Tomorrow." The song was sad as hell, but August Clover was going to cover it, so I needed to make sure I did the music justice. Citizen Shade's tone was crazy rich, too. Deep and soulful. He was one of my favorite under-recognized singers other than Jeffrey James.

I chose a clean black Billy Raffoul concert T-shirt and a pair of jeans, then headed to my bathroom. After flipping the switches for the light and heated floors, I tossed my clothes and cell on the black marble countertop. A plush green towel and washcloth were waiting for me on the heated bar. Ruby was a saint. I had a bad habit of not keeping up with how many clean towels I had in the cabinet beneath the double sinks until they were gone.

Half an hour later, I was awake and dressed. I wiped the steam from my mirror and my blue eyes gazed back at me. Sometimes I stared at myself and wondered who I was other than a son and musician. A heavy feeling of emptiness swept over me, and I placed my palms on the counter. The cool sensation traveled up my arms. Dark thoughts rolled into my mind. What if Mac and Eva had to testify? Would Eva's parents even allow it? She'd been through so much already. That wasn't the only thing I was concerned about, but I shoved the niggling thought to the side. First things first. We had to wait to see if there was any evidence that it was Brandon.

My phone buzzed against the counter, and I scooped it up.

What time are you coming over? Mom just left, so we have the house to ourselves.

I glanced at the clock. It was a little after ten.

I'm going to eat some breakfast, then I'll be over. Have you heard from Eva?

Tiny black dots flickered across the screen, then stopped. I slid the phone in my back pocket since Mac could take a while to respond when she got distracted. I realized her ADHD was difficult for her, but sometimes she was hilarious. Not to mention super smart. Once she found her passion, nothing would stop her. I'd been around her long enough to know how to help her calm down and stay focused for short periods. Most of the time, it was a reassuring touch. For some reason I gave her as much comfort as she did me, but it hadn't always been like that. Not until we were older.

I collected my car keys and wallet off my dresser. The second I opened my door, the smell of bacon and coffee reached my nose. I headed down the stairs and inhaled deeply. Man, I would miss Ruby when I got my own place.

I GRABBED a quick bite to eat, then located the re-altor's business card Dad had given me. Gabrielle was warm and friendly on the phone, and we agreed to meet at the end of the week. For now, she would email listings to me that were cur-rently on the market so she could identify my tastes. Other than talking about it to Dad, I wasn't going to mention that I was house hunting to John, Mac, or Cade yet. I wanted to make sure it would pan out first.

An hour later, I parked in Mac's driveway next to her black Nissan. To her, it was new. Janice had worked her ass off to buy Mac a car for high school graduation, which was in two weeks. Cade, John, and I car shopped with Janice. None of us were too keen on her going by herself. The last thing I wanted was for her to get taken advantage of. We'd found a great deal, and that day Janice brought the car home and put a big-ass red bow on the hood. Saying Mac was giddy when she saw the car was an understatement. I chuckled at the memory of her jumping around and clapping her hands. The only word she could articulate for five minutes was ohmigosh. It was worth seeing her so happy.

I knocked on Mac's front door, then tested the handle. The knob turned, and I swung it open. Mac constantly forgot to lock up after Janice left, but if Brandon got wind that Mac might testify, she would have to be on top of it. The last thing we needed was for him to waltz right in and hurt Mac or Janice. *Dammit.* She had to be more careful. I didn't want to scare her, but we were going to have to talk. I'd never forgive myself if something happened to her. "Mac! I'm here!" I shut the door and flipped the deadbolt into place.

I glanced up to find Mac hanging halfway over the banister waving at me. Janice was constantly on her for leaning on it. If it ever broke … I refused to entertain the possibility. There were times I wanted to roll Mac up in bubble wrap to keep her safe. The girl was reckless.

"That took you forever, dude. Did you have a nice *long* shower?" She wiggled her eyebrows at me. "Come on up." Mac motioned for me to hurry, then she disappeared.

"Who says I showered?" I yelled.

"Your hair is still damp." Mac's giggle echoed through the house.

I slipped off my tennis shoes so I wouldn't drag any dirt inside. Although I helped Mac clean when Janice was at work, I didn't want to track crap onto the hardwood floors. Janice had recently had them restored, and the dark wood had a gorgeous shine to it.

I strolled through the living room to the stairs, then took two at a time to the loft. We had spent a lot of hours with our asses glued to the grey sofa playing video games. Two bedrooms and a bathroom were down the hall. One had been mine for years, and Mac's was next to it. Janice's master was downstairs, which had made it difficult for us to sneak out when we were younger. Janice's hearing was like a moth's. She heard every noise regardless of how soft or loud it was.

I spotted Mac on the edge of the oversized couch with a wireless controller in her hand. Her brown hair hung loose, and she bounced around on the cushions in her black Victoria Secret sweats. Mac was going to town on the Xbox controller buttons. The TV volume was on low. If it was up too high or too quiet, it was a distraction to her. I wondered how she would adjust to life in the college dorm in a few months.

Flopping down next to her, I grabbed the extra controller out of habit. I didn't want to play, though. Mac and I needed to talk.

"Mac, the door was wide open. Anyone could have walked in." I stared at her intently, but she was focused on the television.

"Dammit. I meant to go downstairs when Mom left, and I forgot." She blew a strand of hair out of her face as the sound of her mashing the buttons filled the room.

"Have you heard from Eva?" I wasn't even sure she'd heard me. Mac was entirely absorbed by Alien Isolation. It was an older game, but she loved the challenge.

"Shit!" Mac slapped her palm against her forehead as her character died. Her lower lip jutted out slightly.

"Mac, did you hear me?" I touched her hand, gaining her attention.

Mac's sad gaze landed on mine. "She's not returning my texts. I tried to call, but it went straight to voicemail. I suspect her phone is off." Mac twirled a piece of her hair around her finger.

"I don't know what to do. Should I just go over? I mean the worst that can happen is that her parents refuse to let me in."

I shifted in my seat and draped my arm across the back of the couch. "I don't think that's a good idea. Maybe I can ask Dad to call her father. He seems willing to talk to Dad."

Mac gave me a wistful look. "That's because he's an attorney."

"Sometimes that's to our advantage. If he can get us an update, I'll take it. I know John and Cade are worried about her too."

Mac groaned. "Poor John. He was waiting to ask her out and now we have this shitshow to deal with." She jumped up and turned off the television, the wood floor creaking beneath her heavy footsteps.

"I think we were all holding our breaths to see if she was going to say yes." I slipped my hand into my jean pocket and produced an elastic ponytail holder. Pulling my hair back, I gathered my loose strands and tucked them into a man bun.

"She was going to say yes. She's had a serious crush on John since she was fourteen. Ugh, he wasn't even cute then." Mac giggled as she looked at me. "But you're another story. Girls fucking cream their panties when you wear your hair like that. I never hear the end of it, so maybe you should stop." Mac rolled her eyes and gave me a disgusted look before flashing me a toothy grin.

I threw my head back and laughed.

"You think I'm kidding. Look around you, Hendrix. The more popular the band gets the more the ladies want to scream your name, and I don't mean when you're singing. They're coming out of the woodwork and spreading their legs. Dude, you totally need to get laid. How long has it been?"

My chuckle rumbled through my chest. Mac had never been shy when it came to discussing sex. "Too damned long." I rubbed my chin and mentally counted the weeks since I'd been with anyone. "Months. I guess the last girl I was with was Holly. And honestly, the second the L-word passed her lips we were over. I'm fine with casual, but I don't want a relationship." I held up my hand before Mac could fire a million questions at me. "Before you ask, I was very upfront with her when we hooked up. I told her I wasn't interested in anything other than being friends with benefits."

Mac's mouth gaped, then she wiggled her fingers as she counted them. "Six months?" She waved her hands in front of me. "More importantly. What. The. Fuck?" Mac shook her head. "She said she loved you and you didn't tell me?!" Mac jumped on the couch, then she settled down and tucked her knees beneath her. She chewed on her bottom lip as ran her palm over her thigh and stared at me.

"Yeah. I felt like a total d-bag when I had to tell her I didn't want anything serious. I used signing with the new music label as an excuse. Honestly, it was the truth. I need to stay focused on my career."

"Yeah, I understand it, but. Mmm, no. Fuck that. Get your wick dipped. It's past time for a smash and dash, dude. I'm so down with the idea of a one-night stand and no strings attached. Sounds like heaven to me. An occasional evening of having my brains fucked out so hard I can't walk the next day is the best antidepressant known to the human race. I ..." Regret twisted her features. "Here I am teasing you when Eva was raped last night." Her realization was laced with grief.

"Mac, the difference is consent. If I even got a hint a girl was saying yes out of anxiety or she's not being honest about her feelings. I'm walking away."

"That's part of what makes you different. Too bad I can't clone you, then trade your face for someone else's, so I could date you." Mac snickered.

"Thanks, Mac." I nudged her in the arm with my fist, then a heavy silence hung over us as Eva's name jolted me back to reality.

"Mac," I started, swallowing the lump in my throat. "I need to talk to you about something."

9

My heart skipped a beat. Every fiber in my being scrambled backward, unwilling to have this conversation with her. "If there's evidence that it was Brandon, you and Eva will have to testify in court against him." Agony ripped through me as Mac gawked at me in horror, then she burst into tears.

"I hate Brandon. I fucking hate him." She sobbed into her hands, the vulnerability in her voice splitting my heart wide open.

I closed the gap between us and gently rubbed her back. "I'm sorry. I'm so sorry. I wish I could tell you that everything is going to work out, Mac. What I can promise is that Cade, John, and I will stick close to you. We'll be by your side the entire time. I'm not trying to scare you, but you have to lock the doors, Mac. What if Brandon strolled right into the house? He's dangerous. Please, for me. Lock up after your mom leaves."

"The image you just gave me of that fucker walking into my home ... that did it. It'll stick with me." She tapped the side of her head with her finger. "I promise I'll lock up." Mac peered at me with red and swollen eyes. "I don't know if I can testify, though. Not because I don't want him to pay for what he's done to Eva and other girls ... but ..." Her body shuddered as she cried.

"I'm here." I wrapped her in a big hug and let her snot all over my shoulder.

After Mac's tears ran dry, I released her, and she returned to her side of the sofa.

"I have no idea how this will play out, but I didn't want that dropped on you at the last minute. If I were in your place, I'd need time to process the possibility."

Mac sniffled and she wiped her nose with the sleeve of her pink-and-black plaid shirt. "A part of me will be happy to help put that rat ass bastard in jail. The other part of me ..." Mac chewed on her bottom lip. "I don't understand what happened. He used to not be like this. I mean, right? You're the one that hung around him sometimes."

Memories unfolded in my mind of Brandon and me when our relationship was different. We weren't as close as John and Cade, but we were friends. "He's definitely not the same Brandon. He used to be a good guy." I wondered what had happened for him to make such a significant change. Or maybe I was so busy with the band that I'd missed the signs that he was turning into someone else. A sharp pain stabbed my chest. *What if I could have helped?* I shrugged off the troubling thought. Brandon had always made his own choices even when other people had tried to convince him he was making a bad decision. *He listened to you, though.* I mentally swatted the pesky voice away, but deep inside, I questioned if it was right, and I could have done something to stop him from raping women.

The rest of the afternoon Mac and I kept the conversation light and played video games. It was awesome to hear her laugh and swear like a sailor when I beat her at Mortal Kombat.

"You're such a cheater." Mac pouted and tossed her controller on the floor.

"Someone has to keep your ego in check." I laughed while I stood and stretched. "I need to head out. Text me if you learn anything new about Eva, and I'll see if Dad will talk to her parents and get an update for us."

"Thanks. I appreciate it. And thanks for keeping me company today." She threw her arms around me and hugged me tightly.

"Anytime. Do you have plans tonight, or are you kicking it here?"

"I'm going to go grab something to eat, then come back here and wait for Mom. Maybe I'll go pick up a pizza to cook so she has some food when she gets home after work. One less thing for her to worry about, ya know?"

"She'd probably like that." I headed down the stairs, then slipped on my shoes. "I'll be in the studio with John and Cade. If you get bored, swing by."

"Ohh. I might do that. I can't wait to hear what you guys are working on." Mac bounced on her toes and clapped. She'd been our biggest fan since day one.

"Later." I gave her a wave, waited for the sound of the lock to click, then left. The early evening Spokane sun warmed my face as I walked to my car and pressed the button on the key fob to unlock the doors. Although I hated to admit it, Mac was right. I would love to blow off some steam and get laid, but I wasn't mentally in the place to engage a girl emotionally. It would be strictly physical. Now that the band was growing in popularity, sleeping with the wrong girl could get me into trouble. One wrong word from her mouth, and it would kill my career before it even took off.

I climbed into my car and started it. It was too bad that Cade hadn't grasped that concept. John and I gave him shit about keeping his dick in his pants, but it didn't seem to faze him. It wasn't that I was opposed to hooking up. I wasn't. After watching Dad screw up his marriages and having to take care of him, it had flipped a switch inside me. There were times I wondered if I'd ever find the right girl to settle down with. If I did, she'd have to be a hell of a strong person to handle my past. I suspected I'd never want to share the parts that I'd buried so deep inside myself I wasn't sure if they would ever see the light of day. Some secrets you kept locked up tight because you knew if one of them surfaced, it had the power to destroy you.

I backed out of Mac's driveway and headed toward the college studio. Music had been my salvation, but with Brandon and the FBI's recent actions, I needed another outlet. Maybe it was time to get back into the boxing ring.

My ATTENTION DARTED around the small white room as I entered the studio. One of these days I was going to paint one of the walls bright blue just to have some color other than the console. The space felt sterile and didn't boost the creative energy, but it was the only available option for now, and I was grateful.

"Hey, man," John said as I joined him and Cade in the college studio. "Any word on Eva?"

My chest tightened. All of us were upset, but John was head over heels for her. I couldn't imagine how much this was tearing him up.

"No. I promise I'll let you guys know as soon as we hear." I spun the chair around and sat down. The seat at the console had become mine simply because I understood the controls.

"And Mac?" Cade's lips thinned and he stretched his long legs in front of him.

Irritation bristled inside me. Why was he asking about Mac all of a sudden? I realized he cared about her. We all did. She was one of us, but there was something else in his tone… something I couldn't identify. I clamped down on my frustration.

"She's doing the best she can. I hung out with

her most of the day. We talked about Eva a little bit, but there wasn't much to say. I think all of it was said last night." I didn't want to talk to them about the possibility of Mac and Eva testifying against Brandon. I was sick and tired of that ass-hole taking up my time. Right now, I needed to focus on the new song we were working on.

"I tried to text Eva, but I didn't get a response." He shook his head, wearing a faraway expression. John rifled through a notebook and produced some sheet music. "Here." He placed it in front of me while he ran a hand through his blonde hair. The shit with Eva was wearing on him.

"She was going to say yes." I glanced at Cade, then back to John. "Eva was going to say yes when you asked her out."

A huge grin eased across John's face. "Really?"

"Dude, you didn't know she liked you?" Cade chimed in. "When we're all in a room together, she only sees you."

I chuckled. "Cade's right. But I get it. Even when you suspect a girl is into you, there's no guarantee she'll go out with you."

"I've never been able to figure that out either." Cade frowned and crossed his arms over his chest. One of Ozzy Osbourne's eyes peeked at me from Cade's shirt. Cade and his mom were huge fans of '80s and '90s music. "Like if they're flirting and giving you the signal." He gave a half shrug. "To me it's simple. You like me, or you don't."

"Girls don't think like that." John grabbed a chair next to me, his drumsticks in one of his hands.

"I agree, but let's get this song written and recorded." I was ready to dive in and get my mind off my life.

Unfortunately, our focus was lousy that evening. We finally called it a night at seven thirty. Part of it was my fault because I couldn't shake the uneasy feeling burning through my veins. I even tried the techniques my therapist had taught me, but it hadn't helped.

I entered Dad's house and poked my head around the large white column that marked the living room's entryway. It was more relaxed than the formal living and dining room area located across the white-and black-marble hallway. Sometimes I felt as though we lived in a museum rather than a home.

Not seeing Dad, I spun the key ring around my finger and strolled down the hall in the direction of his office. The door was open, and his voice carried toward me. I tipped my chin up at Charles, who stood with his hands folded in front of him near one of Dad's bookshelves. He wore another black polo and black slacks. I wondered if he owned anything else.

"What?" Dad shot out of his chair and papers scattered across his desk, then fluttered to the floor. The color drained from his face as he half-assed straightened the mess.

"We'll be right there. Hendrix just walked in."

Panic ripped the air from my lungs. "Dad, what's wrong?"

10

"Charles, please pull the car around front." Dad smoothed his blue-and-white checked button-down and finally glanced in my direction. "Brandon," he said in a low tone, the muscle clenching in his jaw.

"What did he do? Dad, what happened? Is it Eva?"

Dad passed me and hurried down the hall. I fell into step behind him.

"You'll need something warm to wear." Dad flung open the coat closet and tossed my fleece jacket at me.

"Dad, what the hell is going on?" I didn't try to disguise the irritation in my tone.

His chest heaved, then he released a long

breath. "Sorry, son. I'm livid and trying not to take it out on you. Brandon … that son of a bitch attacked Mac."

My keys clattered to the floor, and ice flowed through my veins, rendering me momentarily immobile. "Is she okay?" My voice sounded foreign to my ears.

Dad peered out of the window near the front door. "Hendrix, we need to go. Charles has the car ready. I'll explain everything on the way."

He placed his arm around my shoulders and guided me outside. Once Dad locked up, we hopped into the backseat of the Mercedes.

Dad gave Charles directions, then he rubbed his chin. "Brandon is going to be more of a problem than I anticipated."

"It would help if I understood what was happening. Is Mac okay?" My patience was growing thin. I needed to know what the hell had happened and if she was all right.

Dad peered out of the passenger window. "I think so, but I'm not certain. Janice was speaking so fast it was difficult to understand what she was saying." Dad shifted in his seat and looked at me. "Mac told Janice that she was headed out to buy some pizza for dinner. She took the back roads to avoid traffic. The next thing she knew, a car sped around her on double yellow lines, slammed on the brakes, and stopped sideways in front of Mac. She nearly hit the vehicle."

"That sorry son of a bitch."

Dad nodded. "He took a bat to the front windshield and driver's side window. Glass sprayed all over Mac, then Brandon reached in and grabbed her by the neck. According to Janice, he said if she testified against him, he'd kill her."

I curled my hands into fists as white-hot fury swirled beneath my skin. I attempted to regulate my racing heartbeat as images of Brandon's mangled and bloody body rushed through my mind. He was mine. "Dammit. Do you know if she's hurt?" A growing sense of apprehension nagged at the back of my mind.

Dad's intense stare landed on me. "I would think she would have some minor cuts from the window, but other than that we'll have to see. I do know she's terrified. Son, if you're not with Cade or John, you need Charles with you."

"No. You hired him because there's a threat against *you*. Charles is your shadow not mine. I'm not afraid of Brandon. I've knocked him out more times than I can count in the ring. I won the state boxing champ title for three years in a row, remember? I've got this."

Dad rubbed his chin. "I'll agree with you for now. If there are any more situations, I'll contact the company and ask about additional security." Dad fell silent for a moment. "Mac called 911 as soon as Brandon left, then Janice. Janice was at the scene when she reached out to me."

"Thank God she's not alone. If he came back …" My nostrils flared, and I entertained all the ways I wanted to inflict pain on that piece of shit. "How does he think he can get away with threatening her? He has to know she's going to call the cops."

"The police will talk to him, but there's no proof he did anything to Mac. It's her word against his. Unfortunately, his father, Dillon Montgomery, has a lot of pull in Spokane."

No way was he saying what I thought he was. And when did Dillon Montgomery become powerful? I hadn't kept up with Brandon's dad in years since I didn't know him well.

"He has deep pockets and a lot of connections." Dad propped his elbow on the car door.

"And so do you. … or you did. I'm not sure if you burned those bridges or not." I mentally hoped he hadn't. Mac might need more than Dad's help, and Brandon had to be taught a lesson. Put in his place behind bars, preferably.

Ten minutes later, Charles parked the Mercedes on the side of the road. Dad and I jumped out of the vehicle. The blue and red lights cut through the darkness as shards of broken glass crunched beneath my tennis shoes. Mac stood next to Janice while they talked to a female cop. She hugged herself, her shoulders hunching forward.

I shrugged out of my jacket and made my way to Mac. Without a word, I placed it around her petite frame and took her trembling hand in mine. Mac glanced up at me, and I was sure everyone around us could hear my heart shatter. Mac wasn't just scared. She was terrified. Her brown eyes said more than words would ever be able to articulate, even for her.

Remaining as calm as possible, I stayed next to Mac as she rattled off Brandon's license plate number to the cop. I mentally cheered her on for having enough clarity to memorize it. Footsteps scuffed against the pavement behind me, and I peeked over my shoulder. Dad was busy taking pictures of Mac's car as he chatted with a male officer. Although Dad hadn't practiced in a while, it appeared he'd somehow maintained excellent contacts and connections. Everyone liked him. He never pulled any shit. He was a straight shooter and well respected. It was at home where there was a problem. I wasn't even sure how he'd kept his alcoholism under wraps, but he had.

"We'll be in touch, Mackenzie. Are you sure you don't want a paramedic to check you out?" the female officer asked as she flipped her little notebook closed.

I suspected that Brandon's case was closed exactly like the officer's notepad. It was Mac's word against his, just like with Eva's case. From what Dad said, Dillon Montgomery had powerful ties, which meant he might have friends on the police force.

A loud beeping noise broke through the hushed chatter. Mac spun around and slapped her hands over her face as a tow truck backed up to her Nissan. "My car." She groaned and threw her hands up in the air.

"It's not totaled," I said to Mac as Janice led the officer over to the side and continued to chat.

"Thank God, but I don't have … Mom and I don't have the money to fix the windshields." She walked to the car, and I followed her.

"Don't worry about it, Mac. I'll take care of it."

Mac shook her head. "You can't …" She huffed and placed her hands on her hips. "You can't fix everything, Hendrix. I know you want to help, but I'll get a job. School is out in a few more days so I can work over the summer."

"How are you going to get back and forth to a job?" I challenged her.

She frowned and massaged her temple. "Dammit. I live too far outside of the city for public transportation."

"Yeah, I figured. Tell you what. I'll loan you the money to get your car fixed. While they're working on it, get a set of tires. Yours are almost bald. I'll cover the costs, then you can pay me back a little at a time. There's no rush. I've got money saved up from the band's gigs."

"Ugh. I hate needing help, but there's no way around it, is there? I know for a fact Mom's tight on cash." Mac peered at me from the corner of her eye and sighed. "Fine. But once I get a job, I'll sit down and make a budget with Mom and I'll set up a payment plan."

I couldn't help but grin at her. "Even the strongest people need help sometimes, Mac."

"I hate it," she mumbled. "Thank you." She punched me lightly in the shoulder. "Are you going to find Brandon and take the motherfucker down?"

She knew me too well. "Let's talk about it when there aren't cops around." I winked at her.

We stood in silence as the tow truck loaded Mac's Nissan, then left the scene. Once the side of the road was clear, Mac gasped. "Holy mother-fucking shit balls!"

I groaned and gently placed my fingers over Mac's mouth. "Mac, keep it down when we're in public."

She glared at me and pulled my hand away. "Who is that hottie across the road with Franklin? Oh. My. God. It's dark but I can tell from here he's gorgeous. Where did he come from? Has he been here the entire time? He knows Franklin?"

I barked out a laugh. "That's Dad's bodyguard, Charles."

Mac gawked at him, slapped her hands over her mouth, then dropped them as a bewildered look crossed her face. "B-bodyguard?" she whisper-yelled. "Why does Franklin need security?"

I folded my arms over my chest, my attention on Dad and Charles, who were talking to each other quietly. "I have no idea. All I know is that the FBI was there when we arrived home late last night."

"Dude, you're in so much trouble for holding out on me. The *FBI*? What did Franklin do?"

Mac's foot tapped against the road impatiently as she folded her arms across her chest too.

"He won't tell me, but it warranted hiring Charles. He promised me he hadn't done any-thing wrong." A soft breeze blew strands of my hair in my eyes, and I tucked them behind my ear.

"Do you believe him?" Mac peered at me. I assumed she was trying to read my expression, but Dad had taught me well, and I cloaked my concerns from her. She had enough to worry about.

Honestly, I'd asked myself that question count-less times in less than twenty-four hours. At one time, Dad had lied constantly, but it was around his drinking. I'd never caught him being dishonest about anything else. The keyword was *caught*.

"Yeah. I believe him." I rubbed my hands to-gether, catching a chill. "Did you know he's been sober for a year?"

Mac's mouth opened and closed while she struggled for the right words. "No shit? That's ... Hendrix, that's *huge*. Even if he fell off the wagon tonight, which I don't want him to, obviously, it's still a big deal. He couldn't make it through the day without a fifth or three. But you experienced all of this. You were there, so I don't know why I'm rambling on about it."

I draped my arm around her shoulders. "Because you're scared. What Brandon did tonight was fucked up, Mac. It's okay not to know how to deal with it. It's okay to admit he fucked you up."

I glanced down at Mac. Her chin was trembling, and she clenched her teeth. "I refuse to cry, Hendrix. Not here, not where Mom can see."

"Give yourself permission to feel exactly how you feel. There's no shame in it." I gave her braided pigtail a gentle tug.

"Listen to you. A few years of therapy and now you're coaching everyone else." She flashed me a toothy grin.

"Damn straight." I pulled her in for a hug and kissed the top of her head.

"Mac," Janice said from behind her.

"Yeah, Mom?" Mac released me.

"We should get home." Janice offered me a sad smile. "Thank you for coming, hon."

"Always." I embraced Janice, then watched them get into Janice's car, the taillights blinking in the darkness as they left. Red-hot anger pulsated through my veins and my heart rate quickened as I stared at the shards of glass scattered across the road. If I didn't do something to release the pressure valve soon, I was going to blow.

I hurried over to Dad and Charles. "We're seven miles from the house. I'll meet you there." Before Dad could respond, I took off running. Everything inside me screamed that I was acting stupid. First, my clothes weren't appropriate for jogging at night. My jeans and jacket were navy. The only white on my body was my Nikes. Plus, it was fifty degrees out and dark, but I didn't give a fuck. If I didn't rein my temper in and gain control, I'd end up in jail before Brandon, and that wasn't going to happen.

When I was boxing competitively, running long distances was part of my training. I missed it. I missed the sting of the cold air against my skin, the steady slap of my feet against the ground, and my arms propelling me forward. There was freedom in the rhythm.

I hadn't run in a while, but I guessed I was still good for a ten-minute-or-less mile. Since my anger was fueling me, I estimated I'd make it to Dad's in an hour. Images of pummeling Brandon's face with my fists danced through my mind. Mac was trying to be brave, and I loved her for it, but Brandon wrapping his big hand around her throat … I swore under my breath, picking up speed. I needed to clear my head, or I'd end up skulking behind the bushes at Brandon's house, waiting for him.

Focusing on the sound of my breathing, I leaned into the feeling of running—the freedom, the healing, and the sanity it always brought me.

Fifty-eight minutes later, I opened the front door of Dad's home. Sweat trickled down my spine as I wiped the perspiration off my forehead with the back of my hand. I headed to the kitchen and straight to the refrigerator, where I grabbed a bottle of cold water. Once I'd drained it, I leaned against the counter and finally noticed Dad sitting at the table. The moon cast an eerie glow over him, startling the crap out of me.

"Son, we should talk."

11

"Kind of wish you'd let me know you were sitting there when I came in." I tossed the empty plastic bottle into the recycling bin.

"I did, but I think you were too preoccupied and didn't hear me." Dad stood, flipped on the overhead light, and his blue eyes tightened. "I'm worried about you."

I straightened with a jolt as his words hit me in the chest, cracking me open. I was twenty years old, and I never recalled him mentioning that he was concerned about me. We were having a lot of firsts lately.

"Yeah?" I wanted to tell him it was too late for him to be concerned about me, but I realized I would just be lashing out at him. It was nice to hear him say it. How he followed up on his words might be another story, but I needed to give him a chance. After all, he was helping Mac.

"You have a lot on your shoulders to deal with. I was thinking in order to help you process your anger, a healthy outlet would be good." He rubbed his chin, appearing deep in thought. "Alcoholism and bad tempers run in the family, and I don't want to see you make the same mistakes I have."

If I hadn't been leaning against the counter, I suspect I'd have staggered backward. Dad never talked about his drinking problem. Hell, he never spoke about my grandparents. I'd never met them, and it was by accident that I found out what they even looked like. I'd stumbled across a worn picture of them in Dad's dresser when I was eleven. The only way I realized it was his parents was because he'd scribbled on the back of the image. My family were ghosts to me. Mom had left when I was three, so there weren't any connections on her side either.

Since Dad had spent so many years drunk, Janice had talked to me about the possibility of it being hereditary, but she never busted my chops when I had a beer or two. It wasn't often anyway. When you watch a parent drink themselves into oblivion and have to clean up after them day in and day out, drinking until you're stupid loses its appeal most of the time. On occasion, I'd considered losing myself in a fifth, but the second I opened it, images of cleaning Dad's puke and trying to get him to bed dogged my memories. No, thank you. There was no way I wanted to be a burden to someone else.

I stared at Dad, attempting to assess the temperature of the situation. Worry lines were etched into his forehead. He wasn't bullshitting me. He was genuinely concerned. Warmth flooded my chest, and I swallowed the lump in my throat. "Me too," I confessed. "It's why I ran home. I realize Brandon isn't worth going to jail over, but damn." I clenched my fingers into tight fists.

Dad nodded, staring at my hands. "Have you considered hopping back into the ring? It's excellent training and discipline. It was always a good outlet for you."

"Yeah. I might." I looked down at the tile floor, then at him again. "I can work out here for now. I should at least get back into a daily routine. Hitting the bag should help blow off some steam, I don't want to compete again though. August Clover is taking off, and I prefer to stay focused on my music."

"That makes sense. Why don't we go into the living room where it's more comfortable? I have some other things I'd like to share with you."

My muscles twitched as I was consumed with a feeling of restlessness. Dad had my attention for sure. I wondered if he would tell me why the FBI had been here and what they wanted.

I grabbed another bottle of water, then followed him.

Dad sat in the black leather wingback chair and crossed his legs while I stretched mine out on the sofa. My ass was tired after running, but it had deflated my temper, which had been the goal.

"I realize I've never talked to you about your grandparents. It's time you learn the truth, Hendrix." He tapped a finger on the arm of the chair before he continued. Dad was a pro at hiding his emotions, but I'd learned to pick up the small telltale signs when he was stressed or upset.

In one swift move, I placed my feet on the carpeted floor. "Dad, I've asked about them for years. Why now?"

"You're old enough to digest what I'm going to tell you and understand who they are ... were. Also, I'm sober." His voice trailed off, and he folded his hands in his lap as guilt flashed in his eyes. "You're aware that alcoholism, along with other traits, can run in the family, but we have choices. We can choose to walk down a different path. DNA doesn't define us, son. You're grounded enough to understand that."

"I'll take that as a compliment." I leaned back against the couch, wondering what had spurred this conversation on.

"It's meant as one." Dad hesitated briefly. "When I was twelve, some friends and I were out one summer evening. I remember that night like it was yesterday. The crickets were louder than normal, and the full moon was so bright we didn't need flashlights. It wasn't a typical spring evening in Hillsboro, Oregon at all. Most days it was raining so when there was a dry one, we took advantage of it. We were typical boys who explored a lot and got into trouble." A grin pulled at the corner of Dad's mouth.

"There were four of us that were close: Bobby, Jimmy, Sam, and me. Since we lived in the country, we walked on the dirt roads and cut across pastures to get to each other's houses. All of our parents warned us to stay away from Ollie Fisher's place, but they never said why."

"Let me guess, you went there that night." I stifled a chuckle. I'd always wanted to learn about

Dad as a little boy. Apparently, he was ornery, but I wasn't surprised.

"We did. Ollie's family had an old barn, and Bobby talked us into checking it out. It hadn't occurred to us that we would be trespassing. We were just kids, and we rarely thought our decisions through. Anyway, we snuck over to the property, but when we got close to the barn, we heard a scream." Dad swallowed hard, his Adam's apple bobbing in his throat. "The other guys pushed me forward, so I crept up to the door and peeked in through the crack." He stopped and shook his head, a faraway expression on his face.

"What did you see?" I asked softly.

"The lights were on inside the building and I had a clear view. I wish like hell I hadn't." He shifted in his seat, obviously uncomfortable flipping through the Rolodex of his dark memories. "Let me back up a minute. Word had traveled through gossip and the newspapers about an eleven-year-old little girl that had gone missing from Idaho."

My stomach seized, and bile swam up to my throat, nearly choking me. "Jesus. Dad, you don't have to say any more."

Dad held his hand up. "I need to get through this, but I'll keep it brief. That night I witnessed

Ollie's father murder that young girl." His voice hitched and he paused momentarily. "I tried to run, but my feet were rooted to the ground. I was frozen in terror. After hearing another scream from her, my friends took off running. I was the only one left, witnessing every horrid detail of what that monster did to her."

Tears glazed my eyes, and I shook my head, swallowing them down. "I had no idea. I'm so sorry, Dad."

He cleared his throat and pulled in a deep breath before he continued. "Once he'd finished and her limp body lay still on the ground, I bolted. I had no clue I could run that damned fast. I hightailed it home and called the police. Thank God Dad was passed out on the couch and Mom was next door. I wasn't ready to tell them what I'd seen yet."

"Grandpa was passed out?" I placed my elbows on my knees, waiting to learn more about my family. Whether it was good or bad, these pieces that Dad was sharing made so much sense.

"He was a mean drunk, son. Mom and I took turns getting our asses beat. I was more terrified of him than I was of Ollie's father."

Shit. Dad had said his childhood was rough, but I had no idea he'd suffered abuse.

"The cops arrested Ollie's father, and they found the body of the little girl. The evidence was everywhere. I was a hero for finding her. Even my father was proud of me. What I hadn't realized was that I had to testify against a murderer. Ollie's dad would sit in court and I'd stare straight at him and relive everything I'd seen that evening. The nightmares plagued me until I was afraid to close my eyes at night. I'd wake up in a cold sweat, yelling at the top of my lungs. Mom couldn't console me, and Dad … well, he had his own ways of coping with life. One night, he got the big idea to give me a beer. We sat on the porch and drank together. It was one of the few times I ever felt close to him." Dad's shoulders slumped forward, and defeat danced across his expression.

My mouth opened and closed like a fish out of water, the horror of what he'd shared sinking in slowly. "You started drinking at twelve?" What parent hauled their kid into hell with them? My throat tightened as soon as the thought formed in my head. Dad had jerked me into his nightmare, too. Exactly like his father had him.

Dad's cheeks reddened at my comment, then he continued. "Yeah. It stopped the nightmares for a while. I was more relaxed and able to sleep.

Dad and I started a nightly ritual. When the dreams came back, Dad gave me an extra beer. I became his drinking buddy. He was nicer to me and to Mom, so in my young mind it was the best thing for the family. I was protecting us."

I couldn't even articulate how fucked up that was. No wonder Dad hadn't ever talked about it. I suspected he remembered every horrible minute that he saw. If anyone understood what that was like, I did. "Did Ollie's father go to prison?"

His expression revealed a hint of anger and sadness. "The charges were dismissed." The air around us thickened and Dad inhaled a deep slow breath as though he were mentally reliving every second of the nightmare.

"What?" A punch of disbelief and disgust hit my chest.

"I never had to testify against him. Even at that age I understood that the cops or someone in the community was covering up the murder. Ollie's father walked away a free man. I remember Mom telling me the news. I never fell asleep that night, and in that moment, I made the decision to become an attorney. A damned good one at that."

"I always wondered why you chose that career." I released a soft sigh. Dad's life was making so much more sense now. I wasn't willing to excuse his behavior, but it helped me understand him more. A flicker of compassion ignited inside me.

"The people in the area were furious. It only took a few weeks before Ollie's family was harassed and driven out of town. I have no idea where they went, but I was relieved." Dad swung his crossed leg gently in front of him.

"What about Grandpa? I'm guessing the progression lasted a few months and you were drinking every night by then, right?"

"Yeah. The pattern was set in motion and my guilt kept reminding me it was my job to keep Mom and me safe. If it meant having a beer or two with Dad, then I would. Mom was a good person. I saw a spark of light in her again. Dad had beaten her for so long, it had crushed her soul. She was a shadow of the mother I remembered. Until ... until I started spending the evenings with my father."

I collapsed into my seat, and my head buzzed with churning emotions.

"I figured since the alcohol was only at night it wasn't hurting anything. As the years went by, I graduated to the hard stuff. I missed a lot of days my senior year, but I was the valedictorian of my class, so it was overlooked. Once I was accepted into law school, I attempted to stop. At first I sat with Dad on the porch, but it was clear he didn't support my decision. He started in with digs about me wanting to become a fancy attorney, saying that I'd leave my family behind. I tried to assure him I'd buy them a nice house and make sure they had everything they needed, but deep down inside, I wasn't sure if it would turn out like that."

Silence filled the space between us, and I attempted to process what he'd shared with me.

"Although I attended college in Portland, I was required to live on campus my first two years. Honestly, I was relieved. I went home on the weekends for a while, but Dad's drinking and abuse had grown worse. I begged Mom to leave, but she made excuses for him. Finally, I had to make a decision. If I wanted to build a life for myself, I couldn't go back."

I stared at him, my throat raw and aching from the sudden windfall of emotions. "Dad …" I hung my head, my ears filling with the sound of my heart breaking.

12

"Just like the choice I had to make with you." I nearly choked on the pain of my words.

His jaw twitched, his expression betraying his emotions. "Just like you had to with me. I'm sorry, son. I'm so sorry I put you through hell. When I look back at my life now, I see that we've shared some difficult decisions. It scares me how similar we are. You can't make the same mistakes I have. Please don't lose yourself to your anger. Please," Dad said, his voice cracking with his plea.

"I understand. I have a beer sometimes, but that's it. My music and career are too important to me." I didn't have the heart to tell him that not being like him was my number one priority, but we were more alike than I'd ever realized. It scared the living shit out of me too. The cold, hard truth crushed my lungs, and I struggled to catch my breath. What if Brandon was my breaking point, and I couldn't manage life without losing myself in a bottle? What if August Clover became famous and I was sucked into the drugs and alcohol?

"As you know, I made it through law school. I was an overachiever, but I was drinking heavily by the time I landed my first job. I'd met your mom at a frat party, so she drank right along with me. We were each other's life force, feeding off one another and struggling to survive in a screwed-up world. Once she learned she was pregnant with you, she stopped all of the drugs and alcohol, but I couldn't. I was too far gone."

"What was she like? I don't remember her." Pain stabbed me in the gut. If she'd stayed … if I'd been enough for her to stay. I shook the thought from my mind. I was grown and capable of understanding, at least in a small part of myself, that her leaving had nothing to do with me. It was on her. Who the fuck walked away from their kid when the finances were taken care of, and they had a gorgeous roof over their head? No one that deserved my love.

Dad leaned forward, agony flickering to life in his serious expression. "I would really appreciate it if we could save her for another time. It's not been easy sharing this with you tonight."

It wasn't the answer I'd hoped to hear, but I understood firsthand how pulling up horrible memories drained you. "Of course. I appreciate you telling me what you already have." I fiddled with a string on the sleeve of my black polo shirt. "Can I ask what happened to Grandpa and Grandma?"

"They passed away. Dad died of cirrhosis. Mom had a few years left after he moved on. You were two when she died. I reached out to her, but she was empty inside. As hard as I tried to reconnect with her, it wasn't working. While she was on her deathbed ... her final words before she ..." Dad scrubbed his face with his large hands, attempting to hide the tears in his eyes. "I've never told anyone this before, Hendrix." He cleared his throat before he continued. "Mom finally admitted she had blamed me for the last several years that Dad had beat her. She said I should have stayed home with her and put our family first." His voice was low. Haunted. Guilt clung to every word while his shoulders sagged with the weight of his confession.

I jumped off the couch, infuriated that my grandmother would say something so awful to Dad. "That's bullshit. That's so fucked up. You didn't believe her, did you?" Spittle flew from my mouth as I spoke.

"I tried not to, but it had already been in-grained deep inside me. I left her behind. No way would a good son have left his mother in an abu-sive relationship." The chiseled lines of his face were etched with regret and shame.

"Man, she did a number on you. No wonder you never took me to see her." I sat back down on the edge of the sofa, my knee bouncing anxiously.

"Even if I'd wanted to, which I didn't, your mother said no. She said my drinking was bad enough, and she refused to expose her son to sick twisted people. At the time I had no idea that your mother wasn't aligning her interests with yours either. It's why she left. That's all I can say right now."

I struggled for something to say, anything at all to relieve his pain. I certainly didn't excuse his behavior, but his past explained why he'd made poor choices. "It's over, Dad. All of it is behind you. The only person you're responsible for is you. I'm grown. Just take care of yourself and stay sober. Talk to your sponsor, go to meetings, and make sure you stay fucking sober. Please. *Please*. For me. If you think you can't make it, then do it for me." The second the words left my mouth, the little voice in my head reminded me that I'd never been enough of a reason for him to stop drinking. Ever.

"One day at a time. I'm putting one foot in front of the other, shedding the lies that had sunk their teeth into my spirit and ripped me apart. When I look at you, Hendrix, I'm so proud of you. I know I was a shitty father, but I want to make up for it. I want to provide you with a stable home that you can always come back to. I want to be your biggest fan and supporter in your music career. I can't change all of the horrible things that happened. I wish I could erase the pain it's brought us, but I can't. I hope that the changes I'm making now and over the last year will be enough for a new beginning not only for me but for us."

My heart wanted to say yes, that we could forget the past, but it wasn't that easy. The scars of losing ... I slammed the door on the dark memories that had nearly destroyed me. Dad wasn't the only one making progress. "One day at a time. The longer I see that you're sober and working to heal our relationship, I'm willing to move forward. I'll be honest, Dad, there's a part of me that wants nothing more than for this to work." *Be careful. False hope could eventually destroy me.*

Dad's face lit up. "It's all I needed to hear, son. That there's hope for us." Dad stood and approached me. "Can I give you a hug?"

I ransacked my memories for the last time he'd hugged me, but I couldn't remember. I threw my arms around him and squeezed my eyes closed. For the first time since I was little, I felt as though I had a father, and I liked it—a lot.

Dad shifted back, and a movement caught my attention. "Dammit. Charles, you should make more noise when you're around." I glared at him.

"He's supposed to be quiet." Dad chuckled. "His ability to blend in is why he's one of the best."

An interesting thought formed in my mind, and it might work to my advantage. "Maybe you need to teach me, then." I could use those skills to sneak up on Brandon and beat the shit out of him. Of course I wouldn't admit that's why I wanted Charles to train me. Dad would be all over me.

"If Mr. Harrington isn't leaving for the rest of the evening, then I'll meet you in the gym." Charles looked at Dad, waiting for permission.

For some reason, I didn't think Charles was serious, but maybe working with someone was exactly what I needed.

"I think it's a fantastic idea. I'm home for the night, so you guys go ahead." Dad gently squeezed my shoulder. "I'll see you in the morning."

"Night." It was only eleven, and I usually didn't crash out for a few more hours. Working with Charles would help me feel as though I was taking control of my life again.

"I want to change clothes. I'll meet you in the kitchen in a few minutes."

"I'll change too. I want to make sure I have good movement to throw you down on the mat." Charles quirked a brow at me, and I chuckled.

Five minutes later, I met Charles. I was more comfortable and ready to work out. Charles had changed into basketball shorts. His shirt stretched across his broad chest, his muscles rippling with every move. The dude was ripped, but so was I.

My heart was heavy from the conversation

about Dad's parents, and I softly sighed. I strolled through the kitchen, then out the back door to the pool house and gym. Charles followed me silently.

"Were you in the military?" I asked, attempting to learn details about the mysterious bodyguard that was suddenly in my life.

"I served in the Marines," Charles said, his voice low as we reached the entrance.

I punched in the security code, then turned the handle.

He didn't offer any additional information, and I didn't ask. It did explain why he was so rigid, though. Stoic. I hadn't seen him crack a smile or even come close, but I hadn't spent much time with him either.

"Franklin said you were the state boxing champ for three years in a row. That's impressive." At first I thought he was joking, but his expression was serious and a hint of respect flickered in his eyes.

"Yeah, I was. I miss fighting sometimes. Especially the burn of my muscles and the feeling of accomplishment after a good fight. Even if I got my ass beat, it was still a win that I walked away without brain damage." I chuckled. "At least I don't think I have brain damage."

Charles didn't even crack a grin. "Do you want to box or spar? I'm trained in Krav Maga, too. I've had experience in several different martial art forms over the years."

My brows shot up. This guy was lethal. Kill a man with his bare hands kind of lethal.

"From what Franklin has told me about Brandon, self-defense techniques might be good. Brandon boxed with you, right?"

"Yeah." I strolled past the pool, the chlorine tickling my nose. Flipping on the lights, I entered the gym and walked over to the blue mats covering a quarter of the floor.

"Then he would expect you to throw punches. He's studied you, trained with you. He knows his opponent, and the last thing he'll consider is that you've change techniques on him."

Damn. I liked the way this guy thought.

"If I have to take care of him …" I placed my hands on my hips, my tennis shoes sinking into the mat.

"Then you'll be ready," Charles finished for me.

"I'm ready. I'm ready to teach this motherfucker a lesson. What he did to Mac—" I couldn't finish my sentence. If I ever lost my shit and pounded Brandon, I didn't want any of our conversations to land in court and put me in jail.

"Before we start, I want to set the record straight. Anything you and Franklin do or say while I work for you is kept confidential. It's client privilege."

I barked out a laugh. "Even if I run Brandon over with my car?"

Charles didn't even blink. "Even if you murder someone."

I pursed my lips and scratched an imaginary itch on my cheek as I pondered what he'd just said. "That doesn't seem ethical."

"No one said it was." The intensity of his probing stare was disarming. "But I'm on your side. Don't ever forget it."

IT WAS ALMOST one in the morning by the time Charles and I were finished. My entire body hurt, and my muscles burned like a motherfucker. I felt alive for the first time in way too long. He'd taught me several attack and defense moves, then we boxed a few rounds. It felt damned good to have a qualified opponent. He was quick and didn't telegraph his movements, so it kept me on my toes. I wondered how long Charles would be around, but more than that, I was curious *why* he was here. With his training and confidentiality agreement, he definitely wasn't an ordinary bodyguard. I suspected he was trained to kill just as much as he was to protect. Little did I know that I'd have a front-row seat to the show.

13

The following week passed quickly for me, but not for John and Mac. Dad had spoken to Eva's parents, but on an attorney basis, which left the rest of us in the dark. The only thing Dad had said was that Eva didn't want to see or talk to anyone. I didn't blame her, but it was hard watching my best friends worry.

Mac moped around completely heartbroken. She was quiet for a change as well, but I knew her mind was blowing through worst-case scenarios faster than Speedy Gonzalez ran from Sylvester the Cat. Eva and Mac had been inseparable since they were ten. I hated to think that their friendship might be over, but grief took shape in strange ways. Often someone didn't behave the way people thought they should.

The one thing I'd looked forward to was viewing the properties that Gabrielle had emailed to me. It had taken my mind off Eva and Brandon for a little while, and I was enjoying learning what I liked and disliked in a home. So far, nothing had caught my interest. Since I wasn't in a rush, time was on my side, and I could choose my place carefully.

Later that afternoon, I joined John at the guesthouse and waited for Cade to come over.

"Sup?" Cade asked, entering the foyer. He never knocked when he came over, but Cade always texted me when he was on his way.

"Hey, man." I nodded at him as I opened the fridge and grabbed three beers. "Nice shirt." I grinned at his bright orange Janice Joplin tee. After I removed the caps, I handed one to Cade, then joined John on the couch and offered him a Heineken.

"Thanks," John said, taking a drink. "Any news about Eva or Brandon?" He leaned back in his seat and rested his ankle on his other knee.

Cade's gaze narrowed at the mention of Brandon's name.

"Yes," Dad said, walking in unannounced. His

guarded expressions zeroed in on us. He slipped a hand into the pocket of his navy slacks while he walked toward me. I wondered if he carried his one-year sobriety chip in there all the time. Hopefully it provided him some strength and comfort.

Sobriety. Dammit. We all had beers, and since he hadn't knocked, I didn't have time to hide them. The only thing I could do was act casual. I didn't want to embarrass him in front of the guys.

"I just got off the phone with Eva's parents." Dad ran a hand over his dark hair. "There is DNA evidence. The police will request that Brandon submit a sample to see if it matches."

"If it does?" I asked, willing my stomach to stop somersaulting. I wanted Brandon to be held accountable, but at the same time Mac and Eva would have to testify ... if Eva's family pressed charges.

"If it does, then you three need to stay out of it. Let the cops do their job. Don't confront Brandon. In fact, stay the hell away from him. If you threaten him or worse, it could jeopardize the case," Dad said in a clipped tone, his voice dripping with authority.

"So, we do nothing if he comes after Mac again?" I smoothed my black T-shirt, attempting to control the anger that was simmering beneath the surface and on the verge of turning into a rolling boil.

Dad held his hand up. "*If* anything else happens to Mac—"

"If?" Cade asked, an edge to his tone. "I don't mean any disrespect, but wasn't once enough ... sir?"

Dad placed his hands on his hips, his gaze bouncing between John, Cade, and me. "I know this is difficult, guys, but I need you to trust me. I've already talked to Janice and Mac, and we have safety protocols in place."

My nerves were standing on tiptoes. "Security?"

"If it comes to that. I want to make sure that Mac and Janice are safe. I wanted to hire someone today, but Janice asked me not to. She said having a bodyguard around would bring even more unwanted attention to Mac at school. Janice bought tasers and pepper spray for both of them, though. Since I'm not Mac's father, I can't overturn Janice's decision. I have to respect her wishes whether I agree with her choice or not."

"Do we know how Eva handled the information?" John asked, leaning forward in his seat.

Dad's expression filled with compassion. "Not

well. She's been crying all day. Her father contacted Eva's doctor to see if he could prescribe something to help with the anxiety."

John stood and stared at the floor, then at Dad. "Franklin, if I could talk to her, I could assure her that we're keeping tabs on the situation." John held his hand up before Dad could speak. "She doesn't need to know that we're staying out of it, but she needs to feel safe."

"She's always felt safe with John," Cade added, supporting his best friend.

A frown furrowed Dad's brow. "John, were you two involved? What am I missing?"

"We weren't dating … yet. Her parents wouldn't allow her to go out with me until she was eighteen, which was yesterday."

"They've been into each other for a while," Cade informed Dad.

Shit. No wonder John had been down. "I completely forgot her birthday with all the drama going on."

"It wouldn't have mattered. I highly doubt Eva wants to celebrate." Cade plunked down on the couch and stretched his long legs in front of him.

"John, I'll relay your message to Eva's parents and see if she might call you. It's the best I can do."

"Thank you. I appreciate it." John sat down again.

"I'll keep you guys updated. I promise. I know this has been difficult on everyone," Dad said.

My phone chimed, and I located it on the end table. Mac's text flashed across the screen.

My car is fixed! Can I hang with you and the guys? I need some company.

Dad's attention landed on me. "I need to run some errands, but I'll be back shortly. Charles will be with me, so keep the doors locked and the security system set," Dad said.

"Okay. Mac is on her way over. Her Nissan is fixed. We'll probably head to the game room." I glanced at John and Cade.

"Sounds good. I can pick up pizza on my way back if you want," Dad offered.

"Mac never refuses pizza." A playful smile eased across Cade's face.

I chuckled. "That girl doesn't refuse *any* food."

"Pizza it is. I'll see you all later." Dad gave us a small wave before he left.

After we finished our drinks, we headed up to the main house.

"Man, I hate that your dad caught us when we were having a beer. I bet it's hard for him," Cade said.

"Normally he knocks, and we have a second to hide it, but for some reason, he just walked in this time." Guilt gnawed at me. "John grabbed a six-pack last week. We haven't had anything around for a long time." *It only takes one drink, though.* "I think from now on we should lay low. If we want to indulge, we can go to a bar and shoot some pool, then Uber it home." I chastised myself for not being more careful. Dad never came here, so I thought it was safe.

We all agreed to the new plan, and my unease settled down a little.

Once we were all in the main house, I set the alarm system, and we headed upstairs.

"It's been a while since we played pool." Cade strolled over to the wall and removed a pool stick from the wall rack.

"I'm in," John said, selecting his favorite cue stick and the blue chalk cube.

I connected my phone's Bluetooth to the surround sound and pulled up Spotify. We needed something light and upbeat today. The news concerning the DNA evidence weighed heavily on my shoulders. I wasn't in the habit of breaking promises, but if Brandon fucked with Mac again, I couldn't guarantee there wouldn't be some bloodshed. My cell chimed. Mac was here.

"I need to let Mac in," I said.

Before I could head downstairs, Cade laid his stick on the table and moved in front of me. "I know the code. I'll let her in."

Caught off guard, I nodded. The second he was out of earshot, John laughed.

"What's so funny?" I asked, not really wanting to hear the answer.

"You don't see that?" John grinned, a lock of his blonde hair falling across his forehead.

"See what?" I asked, playing stupid. For some reason I thought if I ignored Cade's interest in Mac, it would fade. Cade loved running after the new shiny thing, and at the moment, it was Mac. *But she's not new.*

"He'll be onto the next girl by tomorrow," I growled. "He'd better be, anyway—Mac's gone through enough with Asher and now Eva. Cade will rip her heart out and dance on it. He won't mean to, but that's the way he is. Oblivious to anyone else's feelings."

"Except his dick's." John stifled his laugh with his hand. "If you want him to move on, then we need to introduce him to another girl. Got anyone in mind?"

"No. My social life is nonexistent other than with you fools." I drug my fingers through my hair. "Shit. Do you think Cade is just bored? Maybe he ran out of chicks to hook up with." My nostrils flared. No way was this going to work for me. "You know what, fuck it. I'll talk to him. She's off-limits for all of us."

John held his hands up in surrender. "I'm not the one you need to worry about."

Mac's giggle rang through the hallway, and I cringed. Although I was happy Cade was a distraction for her and she was laughing, he needed to cool it.

Cade returned to the family room with Mac riding piggyback. I caught myself before I groaned out loud.

"Hey, guys. Thanks for letting me hang. Shit's getting intense, and I desperately needed a diversion." She slid off Cade's back, her feet touching the brown carpeted floor.

I strolled over to her and gave her a big hug. "You're welcome any time. You know that."

"So I'm having fucking nightmares about that pathetic ball sack Brandon. I should release some pent-up energy. Who wants to ..."? She tapped her finger against her chin. "Hell, I don't know what I need. I did, however, bring my bikini. We could swim, right? A good game of chicken sounds fun." Mac wiggled her eyebrows at us.

I didn't miss Cade gulping. He'd seen Mac in a bikini a ton of times, but she'd grown top-heavy over the last year.

"I'm in," John said, replacing his pool stick in the rack. "My swim trunks are in the gym already."

"I think we all have trunks down there," I said, resisting the urge to slap Cade upside the head and tell him to put his damned tongue back in his mouth. "Mac, John, why don't you two go ahead. I need to talk to Cade. We'll catch up in a minute."

Mac shot me a suspicious look, but John slipped his arm around her shoulders and led her into the hall. I poked my head out and watched them descend the stairs. "Don't forget to turn the alarm off before you open the back door," I called after them.

I spun around on my heel, my irritation with Cade reaching a boiling point. Stalking over to him, I reminded myself we'd been friends for years and not to be a total d-bag.

"Dude, what the fuck?" I said, then mentally sighed. So much for not being an ass.

14

———

I made sure to keep my voice down in case Mac came back upstairs for some reason.

"What the hell are you talking about?" Cade straightened to his full height and stuck his chest out as he spoke.

Jesus, was he fucking peacocking over Mac? What the hell was going on?

Even though Cade cleared me by a few inches, I could still take him down in seconds, and he knew it.

A sarcastic laugh escaped me as I squared my shoulders. "Mac. It's *not* going to happen dumbass, so back off."

Cade rubbed his chin, his amber-colored gaze

boring into mine. Prickly tension rolled off him. "Screw that. You don't get to tell me who I'm interested in and who I'm not. Before you say anything else, I'm not into Mac, so fucking chill."

He could have fooled me. "Cut the shit, Cade. Even John thinks you're into her. Asher just put her through hell, and now she's afraid she's losing Eva. Not to mention Brandon attacked her a few days ago. She's vulnerable, man. And honestly, you're better than that. Stop thinking with your dick. Normally you'd never move in on her right now."

Cade gaped at me like I'd reached inside his chest and ripped his heart out.

"If you think I'm playing with her emotions, then fuck you." Cade punched his finger into my chest. "All I'm trying to do is make her laugh, even if it's for a few minutes. I don't know how to help her. I'm not as close to her as you are. John has Eva, and you have Mac." Sadness flickered across his features. "I'm trying to take her mind off the pain." Cade's shoulders slumped, and it finally dawned on me how hard he was taking all of this. "I can't be with you guys at night because of all of my own shit at home. I feel like I'm on the outside looking in, and I just want to make it better."

I blew out a heavy sigh. "I think Brandon is getting to all of us. Sorry I busted your chops. I know you've got a full plate too."

"It's cool. I know you're protective of her, but don't forget the rest of us are too. You guys are my family, and I'd do anything for you all." Cade stepped back, staring at me. "We good?"

"Yeah. Let's go have some fun." I cleared my throat. "Oh, one more thing. Keep your tongue in your damn mouth when she's in her bikini."

A silly grin eased across Cade's face. "Dude, her tits are huge. I can't help it!"

I didn't even hesitate when I punched him in the shoulder. Hard. "Find someone else to drool over." I shot him a scathing glance.

Cade didn't respond, which was probably a good thing. He just rubbed a hand over where I'd hit him. I'd always been protective of Mac, and she'd been there for me time and time again. But he was right. She needed a distraction, and I had to simmer down. After all, Cade was my best friend.

AFTER A FEW HOURS in the pool, I was starving. Dad had arrived with three large pizzas, and we all filed into the house, tracking puddles of water across the tile floor.

"I'll clean up the mess, Dad. Let me get into dry clothes first." I grabbed a pair of shorts and a T-shirt from the laundry room and changed in the adjoining bathroom.

Once everyone was dry, we settled in at the bar and loaded up our plates.

"Thanks, Franklin." Mac grinned at him as she took a big bite of pepperoni pizza. She'd piled three large pieces on her plate already.

Dad chuckled as he eyed her food. "Maybe I should have bought more."

Mac giggled. "I can't help it. You know when I'm super stressed, I eat like crazy. Thank God it doesn't go to my waist or my ass, but apparently it goes right to my boobs. I mean, really? I gain weight in my chest? Wouldn't most women overeat all the time if that were a thing? But I swear my boobs finally decided to fill out this last year, and I went up two cup sizes." She put her half-eaten slice of pizza down and held two fingers up. "Even Mom was surprised. She said I get it from my aunt Wendy." Mac shrugged and took a bite of her food.

Dad stammered, color rising high in his

cheeks as he reached for the appropriate thing to say. "I'm glad Janice is there to help you."

"Me too!" Mac finally slowed down enough to realize John and Cade were staring at her ... then her chest. She groaned and slapped John on the arm. "You guys are my friends, so stop thinking with your dicks."

Unable to control my laugh, it bubbled over. I was so used to Mac's ramblings, but this one was priceless. Dad busied himself at the sink, the back of his neck still pink, waiting for the conversation to change, but I couldn't stop chuckling. Maybe I was finally losing my shit. So much had happened over the last week. It had affected me more than I'd realized. Here I was laughing at crap that wasn't really funny, but at the same time, it was fucking hilarious.

Cade snickered, his cheeks burning bright red. John stared at the floor, then mumbled an apology for ogling Mac's tits. We'd all noticed she'd filled out, but her sharing the details was priceless. It was times like this I loved Mac for having zero filters on her mouth. Other times it was a bit of a challenge to deal with, but we were home, so it didn't matter.

"I'm going to head to the office. Kids, let me

know if you need anything," Dad said, then left the room.

My good mood dropped faster than a lead ball. Something was off. I hopped off my barstool and excused myself. "I'll meet you guys upstairs." I didn't wait for their response.

Had my stupidity with the beer situation earlier screwed with Dad's sobriety? Guilt reared its ugly head as I hurried down the hall to his office.

He hadn't shut the door, but he was facing away from me.

"Dad?" I asked softly, leaning on the doorframe.

"Yeah?" He didn't turn around.

My heart thundered in my chest and my palms immediately grew clammy. Was he hiding something from me?

15

"Are you okay? I'm sorry about the beer earlier. You never go down to the guesthouse, so I didn't think anything about it when I grabbed a six-pack." Technically, John had bought it, but I hadn't objected, so the responsibility was on me.

Dad turned the chair around slowly. "No, son. I hate beer. If I can't have the hard stuff, I won't waste my time."

"I still shouldn't have had it around." I kicked at the beige carpet with the toe of my tennis shoe, then looked at Dad. "I can tell something is wrong. Is it Eva or Brandon?"

"No." He set a manilla file on top of his tidy desk, then flipped it open.

My attention followed his movements and landed on several images.

"After telling you about your grandparents ... It brought up a lot of memories. Over the years, I'd kept tabs on them and hid a few pictures away. It's all I have left now."

I wasn't sure what to say. "Are you wanting to drink? Did talking about all of that mess with your head?"

"It did, but not in the way you're thinking. If anything, it gave me more motivation to stay sober and rebuild my life." He glanced up from the folder. "Actually, it reinforced my path. It was like a bucket of ice-cold water was dumped over my head when I realized the similarities that I'd put you through. I'd had to make the same decisions, and I swore back then I'd never hurt someone I loved the same way that my father had me." A conflicted look painted his face, and an abundance of different emotions stared at me. Guilt. Regret. Anger.

My heart stuttered against my chest. "Yeah, it sucks, but you didn't drink or hurt anyone today. Today is all we have, right?"

Dad nodded.

"Then we'll count it as another win." I wasn't sure what else to say, except that he'd made it through the day, and that was important to acknowledge.

"Yes, we will. Thanks for checking on me, but I'm fine. The longer I'm sober, the clearer my life becomes. It's a welcome change even on the hard days."

Relief flowed through me. My beer hadn't screwed Dad up. At least I'd talked to the guys, and we'd agreed no more alcohol in the guesthouse. I didn't care how much Dad said he only drank the hard stuff. I didn't want it to be available. Maybe down the road it would be different. When I had my own place, I wouldn't concern myself about it unless he was over to visit.

My phone pinged, and I removed it from my back pocket. Spotting the email from Gabrielle, I sank into the chair in front of Dad's desk. "Gabrielle sent me some more properties to look at."

"Is there anything good?" Dad asked. I didn't miss the mixture of eagerness and disappointment in his tone.

I scrolled through the selection. My adrenaline kicked in, and I vibrated with excitement as I scanned the details of one home in particular. "Here's a three-bedroom, three-bathroom house on the Spokane River." I handed him the phone.

"I want to see it. There are two others I'm interested in looking at, but this one ... the sound of the rushing water while we're on the back patio would be amazing." I couldn't stop the grin easing across my face.

"It looks like it could be a great fit. The one thing you need to prepare yourself for is that most of the time, the pictures are better than reality. I'm not trying to discourage you, just attempting to provide some information to help manage your expectations."

"That makes sense. I'm going to let her know there are three I'd like to look at. What's your calendar look like tomorrow?"

Dad didn't even hesitate. "I'm available whenever you can go."

I mentally sifted through my class schedule for that afternoon. Since it was Wednesday, Cade, John, and I wouldn't have the studio, so I was open all afternoon.

"I'll give Gabrielle my schedule and let you know what she says." I typed out a quick email to her, then placed my phone in my lap. "By the way, I've not mentioned any of this to Mac or the guys. I'd like to keep it quiet for now. I have no idea how long it will take me to find something I love."

"I think that's a wise move. The only other

person that will know is Charles. He'll drive us tomorrow, but he won't say anything."

I ran my fingers through my hair. "He's interesting."

"He has a very special skill set. You can feel safe with him."

I picked up my cell, then stood. "I'm going to join everyone in the game room. I'll let you know as soon as I hear from Gabrielle." As soon as I finished my sentence, my phone pinged. I chuckled when I spotted a return email from her. "She's fast. I have to give her that." I tapped the screen and opened the message. "How about two tomorrow?" I peeked up at Dad. "Maybe you and Charles can pick me up from school, then drop me back off to pick up my car."

"That sounds good. Then if your classes run over, you're not in a huge rush. I'll let Charles know."

"Awesome." I flashed Dad a big smile. "Thanks for going with me."

"You bet." Dad flipped open his laptop, and I excused myself.

I bounded up the stairs two at a time, then joined everyone. The speakers reverberated through the game room as Mac and John played Call of Duty on the PlayStation 4. Mac was hilarious to watch. She put her entire body into a game. Suddenly, she jumped off the couch and sank into a squat, moving side to side as she attacked the enemy.

I glanced at Cade as he stood behind the sofa, glued to her every move. He laughed as she kicked John's ass. I couldn't help but chuckle. It was nice to feel happy for a while and not have the weight of the world crashing down on me like a tidal wave.

My earlier conversation with Cade ran through my mind. Even though we went way back, and I'd trust Cade with my life, there was still something a little off. Only time would tell if he really did have feelings for Mac. For now, I'd keep my mouth shut. I had enough to deal with anyway.

16

The crystal blue sky and bright sunshine warmed my skin as I took my time and strolled across campus. The weather had me seriously considering cutting classes—especially the last one of my day, Biology. I had no use for it. It wouldn't assist me in writing music and performing, but for some dumbass reason, it was still a requirement to graduate.

Entering the auditorium-style classroom, I scanned the room for a good seat in the middle. I settled into a chair and placed my books and phone on the desk. A cute girl caught my attention as she walked toward me. She stood about five-seven with long brown hair and blonde highlights. I sat up a little straighter and offered her a smile.

"Hi," she said softly. "Is anyone sitting next to you?" Her light blue top accentuated her big doe eyes.

"Help yourself."

She sat down and settled in. "You're Hendrix Harrington, aren't you?"

I was still adjusting to the fact that people recognized who I was. Most of the time, it took me off guard, but this time I was flattered. "Yeah."

"I'm Andrea Wallace." She stuck her hand out to me.

"It's nice to meet you." I took her small hand in mine. She had a firm handshake, which told me she was confident. Most girls screamed my name and behaved like second graders, but not Andrea. She didn't seem ruffled at all that she'd just walked over and introduced herself to me.

"I hate that we have to attend class inside today. It's so beautiful out." She opened her Bio book and grabbed her notebook and pen.

"After the winter months, we're all eager to get outside. I really think they should have outdoor classrooms. Hell, I'd even sit on the grass."

"Same. It might help me focus better." She giggled softly. "It's pretty bad that I'm majoring in nursing, and I hate Biology."

This girl was different than most. Andrea had shared a wealth of information in a few short sentences. She cared about people, wanted to make a difference, and was eager to step out of the classroom and into her career. I suspected she was driven and passionate as well. I stifled a chuckle. Dad had taught me to listen to the words a person spoke but focus on their body language as well. People could lie all day long, but their bodies would betray them. If you knew what to look for, you could size someone up pretty fast. The tricks Dad had learned in court had served me well too. Most of the time, I'd been spot on. I hoped I was this time too.

Professor Kline entered the room and stood next to his podium. Thank God the class was only fifty minutes, but it was three times a week and packed full.

I buckled down and wrote a ton of notes. Even though I wasn't excited about Bio, I set a standard for myself concerning my grades. I'd study my ass off if I had to, but I wouldn't settle for anything less than a B. With that said, I'd pulled straight A's in my first year of college.

When the class wrapped up, I remained in my

seat and allowed people to pass me. I glimpsed at the clock on the wall. Dad and Charles would be here in half an hour, which gave me a few minutes to chat with Andrea, who hadn't moved from her chair yet.

"I missed part of what he said about the supported facts of climate change. Did you catch it?" She peeked at my notes, then at me.

"Yeah, let me find it." I flipped the page back and found the information she needed. "Here." I handed her the notebook.

"You have really nice handwriting for a g—" Her cheeks pinked. "That was a sexist thing to say. Sorry. Your handwriting is really nice, though."

"For a guy?" I asked, laughing. "That doesn't bother me. I don't get offended easily."

"Good because I didn't mean anything by it." She gave me a quick smile.

I watched as Andrea finished jotting down the information she needed. "Thanks." She returned my notes to me as a sharp scream carried through the hall.

Our class was next to the front door, so I couldn't tell where the cry came from. I grabbed my belongings, then shot out of my chair and over Andrea's legs.

"Help!" the female voice cried again. My first thought was that Brandon had cornered someone, but as I entered the deserted hall, I saw a small crowd outside on the lawn.

"I can't see what's going on," Andrea said from behind me.

I hadn't realized she'd followed me. I slammed against the bar of the glass door, flung it open, then hurried down the stairs.

The crowd was growing but was still small enough that I could see a pair of white tennis shoes pointed toward the sky.

"Oh shit," Andrea said. "Hold these." She shoved her books into my hands and gently elbowed her way through the people. "I'm a nurse. Well, almost, so please let me through."

I squeezed in behind her in case I could help. Andrea dropped to her knees and placed two fingers against Professor Kline's neck.

"Does anyone know what happened?" I asked.

"I was asking him a question, then he just fell to the ground," a dark-haired girl responded.

"He's not breathing. Did anyone call 911?" Andrea asked as she tilted his head back and checked his airways.

"Yeah. They're on the way," the same girl replied.

"Let's move and give Andrea some room." I could help with crowd control, at least. Hopefully the paramedics would arrive soon, but from the looks of it, Professor Kline was already gone. I clutched my books until my fingers turned painfully white while I witnessed Andrea perform CPR. She was calm and collected. It hadn't appeared to faze her that her Bio professor was dead and lying on the ground.

Suddenly, the professor coughed, and his eyes fluttered open. Andrea grabbed his wrist and looked at her watch. "Professor Kline, it's Andrea. Please be still. I suspect you had a heart attack, but I'm not sure."

Professor Kline blinked rapidly and attempted to sit up. "No, lay down." I sat next to him and talked to him quietly as we waited for the ambulance. The best thing I could do was to encourage him to stay calm.

A few minutes later, the sirens filled the air. Paramedics ran over to us, and I backed away, allowing them to help the professor.

Andrea updated the medics, then joined me.

"You were pretty amazing," I said, handing her books to her.

"Thank God I knew what I was doing. If not, I think we'd be planning a funeral." She glanced up at me and sighed. "I never thought the first life I'd save would be my Biology teacher's. I was scared shitless that I wouldn't be able to help him."

"Wow. I had no idea. You seemed super calm." I adjusted my Bio book in my hand. "It's funny how things work out. If we hadn't chatted for a few minutes after class, you would have already been gone."

"It's crazy how that timing worked out, huh?" She gazed up at me, her warm brown eyes making my heart skip a beat.

The crowd had finally cleared out, leaving only a few stragglers.

"I have to go, but I'll see you in Biology on Friday?" I asked.

"Yeah. Save me a seat?" She brushed the grass off the knees of her jeans, then straightened.

"I'd love to." I grinned at her. "But would you be interested in grabbing dinner tomorrow night? It would need to be early because I have the studio reserved at seven-thirty ..."

Andrea tilted her head, "Are you asking me out, Hendrix Harrington?"

I chuckled. "I am."

"What time would work for you?" Her smile lit up her pretty heart-shaped face.

"Five thirty? It will give us a few hours at least. I'm happy to pick you up."

Andrea bit her bottom lip. "Really? I've not had a guy pick me up and drop me off in like forever. We always meet somewhere since not everyone has a car."

I handed her my phone. "Give me your number and address, then I'll shoot you a message, so you have mine too. Well, not my address, I hope you understand."

Andrea laughed. "I do. You're a celebrity. The last thing you need is a crazy girl knocking on your door." She cringed. "That came out wrong. I'm not crazy, I promise." She gave my cell back to me, then I fired off a quick text.

"I'll see you tomorrow." *Holy shit, I had a date.*

I watched as she walked away, then peeked over her shoulder at me. I stood there like a dumbass with a big silly grin. I'd learned not to jump to conclusions about dating someone. Hell, I never even speculated if a relationship would work out or not, but the fact that I was interested enough to ask her out was progress.

Turning toward the parking lot, I glanced at the time on my phone. Dad should be here by now. I jogged over to where we'd agreed to meet. After we checked out the properties, I'd have to fill John and Cade in on Andrea. They'd give me crap about having a date, but I knew they'd be happy about it too.

Spotting Charles standing next to the Mercedes, I hurried over. Before I reached the car, Charles opened the passenger door for me.

"Thanks, man." I slid into the back beside Dad.

"How was your day, son?"

"It started off pretty boring, then it got really interesting." Over the next few minutes, I filled him in on Professor Kline, Andrea's quick and calm reaction, and how I'd asked her out.

"She sounds impressive. Maybe she'll be the right one for you. I do respect how you've not slept your way through Spokane. You're using good judgement, son. I'm proud of the man you've become."

"Thanks," I said, caught off guard with his compliment.

My heart expanded in my chest. I liked this new, sober Franklin.

17

*C*harles parked the Mercedes at the first house on my list. A sweet little black BMW M2 was lined up in the driveway. My attention landed on a well-dressed woman in beige slacks and heels. Her royal blue blouse revealed some cleavage and the sapphire necklace around her neck. She strode over to us, confidence rolling off her in waves. She patted her long dark hair that was pulled back into a sleek bun, the giant diamond ring on her middle finger catching the sunlight as she approached our car.

I hopped out, ready to introduce myself, but Gabrielle made a beeline to Dad.

"Franklin, it's so good to see you." She kissed him on his cheek and took his hand in hers.

"Gabrielle, you look stunning as always. Thank you for helping Hendrix."

She finally looked at me, and her mouth gaped. "Oh my goodness. You're the spitting image of your father."

I chuckled and rubbed my smooth chin. "Lucky me. He's a good-looking guy."

Gabrielle peeked up at Dad. "That he is. Well, we better get started. Are you ready?" she asked me.

"I am." I grinned at Dad. It had been a while since I'd seen a lady flirt with him. Dad took it in stride as though he were used to women falling at his feet all of the time. Maybe he was, and I'd never realized it before.

Dad and I followed Gabrielle inside, but I noticed Charles climbing out of the car before closing the door. I squelched my laugh as he approached the entryway, and I recalled Mac's reaction to him. I wondered how Gabrielle would react.

Charles followed behind me ... silently. It would be best if I let Gabrielle know he was there. He had a bad habit of scaring people.

"Excuse me, Gabrielle?" I asked.

"Yes?" She spun around in her high heels, then screamed.

Shit. "It's okay. I wanted to tell you that Charles is our bodyguard and will be with us today. He's so quiet people aren't aware of him. I was hoping not to scare you." I shot Charles a scathing look.

He stared at me, unflinching.

Dad slipped his arm around Gabrielle's waist as she attempted to recover from the shock of seeing a hulking badass standing behind me. "I'm sorry, Gabby. Are you all right?"

Gabby? Gabrielle's hand fluttered over her chest as heat rose up her neck and cheeks. "Yes, thank you." She smoothed her slacks and regained her composure.

"Pretend he's not here," Dad said.

From the looks of it, I didn't think that would be possible.

Gabrielle bit her lower lip and eye fucked Charles, and I nearly lost it. This was a show I hadn't anticipated.

Dad cleared his throat, jerking her attention away from our bodyguard.

"Yes. Well, let's head upstairs, shall we?" Gabrielle tucked her leather binder beneath her arm and returned to the project at hand, which was selling me a place to live.

Within a few minutes, I knew this wasn't the right one for me. I respectfully shared my thoughts with her, then we left.

The next house was only a few miles away, so I didn't have much time to flip Charles a bunch of shit about an older lady nearly throwing herself at him. I'm not sure Dad would've appreciated it anyway. I'd have to wait until Charles and I were alone.

A half hour later, I'd seen the second home. Even though I liked it better than the first one, I wasn't excited about it. I hoped we'd saved the best for last. Dad had reminded me that searching for the right place took time, and I'd recognize it when I saw the right one.

As soon as we pulled into the driveway of the last one, my heart jumped. This was the property on the Spokane River. I climbed out of the Mercedes and inhaled the fresh air. The clean scent of the water reached me, and my heart soared.

"If you're quiet, you can hear the river rushing by from here," Gabrielle explained.

I stood still and listened. The soft roar filled my ears, and a grin eased across my face.

"I like that smile," Gabrielle said. "Let's go in."

"The trees are beautiful. They shade the front

of the house nicely," Dad said from behind me. His dress shoes scuffed against the asphalt driveway. Charles made no sound at all.

The lights automatically turned on when I stepped inside. "Do we need booties?" I asked, noticing the polished wood entryway floor.

"Yes," Gabrielle pointed to the basket with the blue shoe covers. "Just don't slip on the floors."

My attention bounced from her to the living room with the floor-to-ceiling stone fireplace. Two love seats and a recliner filled the space nicely. A TV hung on another wall, and I mentally envisioned mine in the same place.

"Let me show you the kitchen," she said. The second her foot reached the tile floor, the room lit up.

"Wow, this is gorgeous. I love to cook and have my friends over to hang out, so this would definitely work." I ran a finger across the granite countertop and scanned the oak cabinets. "I'd want to update everything, but the space and layout are great."

I glanced at Dad, who nodded his approval. "You'll definitely want some changes and make it your own, but it's got great bones."

"Let me show you the outdoor area. Gabrielle

flipped open the lock, then slid the glass door open.

"Oh my God," I whispered. I could see the river from where I stood. The rushing water was louder than I thought it would be, the scent of it tickling my nose. I sucked in a deep breath and soaked in the quiet beauty around me. The birds chirped softly in the top of an oak tree, and a huge grin split my face. The patio and yard felt like home. Now I had to figure out if the house would work as well.

"Two bedrooms are upstairs, and one is down here next to the bath in the hallway." Gabrielle led the way while Dad and I followed.

Dad asked a few questions that I hadn't thought of, which made me grateful he was with me. He'd been considerate of my opinions and hadn't inserted his unless it concerned a safety issue. We followed Gabrielle up the stairs and to the master bedroom.

I smiled serenely. The room was huge with an equally enormous en suite bathroom. I strolled over to the floor-to-ceiling windows and whistled. The view was stunning. This corner would make a great sitting area. I could work on music and stare out the window, watching the river rush by in the wintertime. When it was warm out, my ass would be on the back patio.

After seeing the bathroom and additional bedroom, we went downstairs again. I left Dad and Gabrielle chatting in the kitchen while I took another look around. Mentally, I was already moving in and attempting to calculate the cost of the updates I wanted.

I eyed the wall at the end of the hallway. "Hey, Dad?" I called.

Dad and Gabrielle joined me as I gently rapped a knuckle on the painted sheetrock. "I wonder if this spot might work for a studio. I'd have to see how much space is available since it would be an addition, but ..."

Dad folded his arms over his chest. "I think it has a lot of potential. We'll look outside before we leave," he said with a decisive nod.

"If you're interested, Hendrix, I can get the information for you. I can also talk to one of my contractor friends and get him to work up an estimate on adding the studio and the upgrades you prefer. Then, you'd be fully aware of the investment it would take to make this what you want."

"Really?" I asked. Every cell in my body hummed with anticipation. "That would be great." I reminded myself not to get excited yet, but I couldn't help it. The house had serious potential. With three bedrooms, the guys and Mac could stay any time they wanted. The patio was perfect for entertaining, and the windows in the master were heaven.

"Are there any other offers on the table right now?" Dad asked Gabrielle.

"Let me make a quick call to the listing agent, and I'll find out." Gabrielle squeezed Dad's bicep, and he patted her hand before she excused herself.

I stifled my gag and hoped that Dad wasn't interested in Gabrielle. She'd just flirted with Charles in front of him, how could he even consider going out with her? "I want to go back upstairs." I waved for Dad to follow me. "What do you think?" I asked, wanting his opinion in private.

"I think it would be a great place for you. It's close to school and not too far away from your old man." A sad smile eased across Dad's face.

"That's a good thing," I assured him. Walking the length of the master bedroom again, I sighed. "I really like it. With the upgrades, it will be perfect. It's not so big that I can't manage it on my own, too." I chuckled. "Do you think we could share Ruby?"

Dad laughed so hard his chest shook, his eyes dancing with amusement. "Nice try, son. Find your own housekeeper." He patted my back as Gabrielle returned.

"What did you find out? Are there any offers?" I asked, eager for the update.

18

"There are five competitive offers on the table right now."

My stomach plummeted to my toes.

"The owners are accepting additional bids until midnight tonight, then they will choose one. If you want to make an offer, you need to do it today and make sure it's the best you can do."

I scrubbed my face with my hands. This wasn't what I wanted to hear.

"Why don't we go grab a bite to eat and discuss a plan? Gabrielle, do you have time to work out the details with us, or do you have another appointment?" Dad asked.

I swear *Gabby* batted her long eyelashes at

Dad. "I'm yours for the rest of the day," she purred.

No wonder Dad liked her. She was good for his ego.

Before we left, we walked the property and looked at the possible space to add a studio. From what we could tell, it would work.

GABRIELLE, Dad, and I had a late lunch at Clink-endagger's and discussed finances. Once we hammered out taxes and the monthly payment, it was unfortunately out of my price range.

"The band has gigs lined up for the next six months, which means I can double up on the mortgage payments, but I'm not sure how it helps me now." I was trying not to let the disappointment deter me, but it wasn't working.

"Gabby, if you'll excuse us for a few minutes?" Dad pushed his seat back and stood, smoothing his light grey button-down shirt.

"Of course." She beamed at him.

"Son, let's take a walk and discuss business."

Without a word, I scooted my chair back, then joined him. Charles caught my attention in the closest corner of the restaurant. He began to follow us as well.

Once we were outside, I took a deep, slow breath. Clinkendagger's was also on the Spokane River, and the rushing water calmed my nerves.

"I can't afford it yet, Dad. It won't work. I'm trying to look at every possible angle, but I'm coming up short every single time."

"Hendrix, the other offers will most likely be above the asking price." Dad rubbed his smooth jawline, frowning as if deep in thought.

I suspected disbelief was written all over my face. "It's already at the top of my budget, but you're aware of that."

Dad and I walked silently for a moment.

"Let me put in a cash offer for you." Dad stopped and looked at me. "Before you say no, hear me out."

I crossed my arms over my chest and nodded. Dad couldn't buy my forgiveness, and it wasn't for sale anyway. It had to be earned.

"When you were growing up, I didn't provide for you when you moved in with Janice, and you have no idea how sorry I am. But now, I can. I'm sober, we're doing better, and I'd love to do this for you. The money you have saved up would allow you to hire the right contractors to make upgrades and eventually add the studio wherever it would work best. You have almost three-quarters of an acre with a lot of flat land, so you should be able to add it without a problem." He paused. "Hendrix, if it feels like home, then it's the right place for you. Your entire face lit up as soon as we walked into the house and even more when we were outside. Let me help. I want to do this."

I dropped my hands to my sides. "I want to do this for myself. It's my first big purchase, and I wanted to own the process and feel good about the accomplishment." I patted my chest with my hand, indicating it was a heartfelt choice.

Seconds later, the harsh reality sunk in. There was no way I could buy the place without him, and I could see myself living there for a long time. I kicked the sidewalk with the toe of my shoe, my heart and mind in a full-on tug-of-war. Dad wasn't wrong, either. He hadn't provided for me after the age of thirteen. Janice had. On occasion, he'd send her a check, but I was mowing lawns and providing yard work to help pay for my clothes. I'd learned to take care of myself and work at an early age. Maybe accepting his offer meant it was a step forward for us. Plus, it was plain and simple. Did I want this place or not?

Glancing up at Dad, I swallowed my ego. "Okay, I accept your offer. I'll use the money I have saved to have the upgrades done."

Dad's smile reached his eyes, then he grabbed me in a big hug. "Thank you for allowing me to help."

"Thanks for offering." I hoped I was doing the right thing.

"Let's get back inside and work on the offer. I suspect Gabrielle has been doing a bit of research while we've been out here chatting. She might be able to provide some wisdom."

I suspected Gabrielle would be happy to offer Dad something else, but I wasn't going to mention it to him.

The next few hours passed quickly as Gabrielle and Dad agreed on a price that was not only in cash but one hundred thousand over the listing price. I wasn't surprised. This was about more than the home I wanted. It was about Dad trying to make up for being a shitty father. What he hadn't figured out yet was that by simply showing up sober and being a part of my daily life, it carried more weight with me than all of his millions of dollars.

"Okay, I'll send the offer over immediately, then we wait. They'll respond by tomorrow evening. And, Hendrix, I know you want this particular one, but I swear to you, if it falls through, we'll find another one that's even better." She patted my hand and gave me a reassuring smile.

"Thank you. I definitely want a place on the water."

After we said our goodbyes, Dad and I climbed into the backseat of the car, and Charles headed to the school for me to pick up my Camry. I laid my head against the seat and drummed my fingers against my jeaned leg.

"I think the next twenty-four hours are going to seem like an eternity."

Dad sat his phone in his lap and squeezed my shoulder. "Buying a house can be stressful. I do feel confident about our offer, though. However, sometimes money isn't the only factor the seller is looking for."

"I don't think that helped me feel better." I cracked a grin at him. "Well, in the meantime, I have a date tomorrow night, so maybe that will help take my mind off the wait."

Dad's cell rang, and he answered.

"I'm sorry, what?" Disbelief clouded his expression. He glanced at me, worry lines creasing his forehead.

Dammit. What was happening?

19

"This isn't what I was hoping to hear." Dad ran his hands through his hair, anger rippling through him and filling the small space of the car.

Anxiety hummed beneath my skin as I waited to learn why Dad was so upset.

"I'll reach out to Janice and give her the update. Thank you for calling. Please let me know if there's anything I can do for you or Eva."

Dad ended the call and shifted in his seat, facing me. "That was Eva's father." Dad shook his head as though he were still trying to digest whatever he'd heard. "The charges against Brandon have been dropped. There won't be a trial."

I ground my molars, mentally counting to ten before I responded. "How?" I croaked.

"This is what I was concerned about. I suspect Dillon Montgomery pulled some strings because the DNA evidence is gone. It would be Eva's word against Brandon's and her parents don't want to put her through it now that the chances are slim to none of winning the case." Dad pursed his lips. "The only positive thing about this news is that Mac doesn't have to testify. Maybe she won't be on Brandon's radar anymore."

I could only hope. "That son of a bitch gets off on scaring people. If he's not stopped …" Scenarios of his bloody and beaten body danced around in my imagination. He needed to be taught a lesson. Someone had to stand up to him. Although I'd promised Dad I'd stay out of it, that was when we thought charges would be brought against him. It was different now. The piece of shit had just walked away without any consequences.

"My hands are tied, son. I'm so sorry." Dad's words dripped with defeat and stabbed me in the heart. "There's one more thing."

I cocked an eyebrow at him. "Because that wasn't bad enough?"

"Eva and her parents are moving. They want

to offer their daughter a fresh start. She's not sleeping and terrified that Brandon will come after her again."

My throat clogged up. "John and Mac are going to be crushed, but I don't blame Eva's parents for wanting to protect her."

"When she's ready, she'll attend college online. Eva won't ever be the same. I hope she attends therapy and has the support she needs as well," Dad said.

I tapped my fingers against my thigh, attempting to process the news. Deep down, I wanted Eva to heal, but the whole situation fucking sucked. "Me too. When are you going to talk to Janice? I'd like to be with Mac when she finds out. The second she sees me she'll know something is wrong. I won't be able to hide it."

Mac has a great bullshit radar. "That girl could sniff out when I'm hiding things from her even if she was standing in a dark alley full of skunk weed."

Dad chuckled. "She has a sixth sense when someone is feeding her bogus information, that's for sure."

"It's why I never bother. All I need to know is how to help her. She's losing her best friend, and Brandon terrified her."

"You and Mac are my main priorities. I'll do everything in my power to take care of you both. It's my job as a parent."

His promise was so tangible I could taste it on my tongue. He'd planted a seed of hope in my heart. Maybe ... just maybe my dad was finally turning into the man I'd always dreamed he could be.

"Thanks. You have no idea how much that means to me." I stared out the back passenger window as Charles continued to drive. It had been a long day and I was ready to grab my car and head home. Home, what a funny word. For most of my life, it had been an empty shell and full of despair, fear, and loneliness. Never in my life did I think it would ever change.

I RAPPED my knuckles on the guesthouse door. John's dark green Honda Civic was parked in front of the garage, so as far as I knew, John was there.

"It's open!"

Sucking in a deep breath, I walked in, then closed the door behind me. John was sitting on the couch with sheet music in front of him.

"Hey. Are you busy? It looks like you're working." There would never be a good time to tell him that Eva was leaving.

"Nah. I'm just thinking through some beats." He finally looked up at me, his expression growing serious. "You don't look so hot."

I strolled into the kitchen, feeling the nervous tic in my jaw, I pursed my lips.

"Dad heard from Eva's parents about thirty minutes ago. There won't be any charges against Brandon. Somehow the whole entire shitshow got covered up."

John jumped off the couch, sending the papers flying to the floor with his sudden movement. He scrubbed his face with his palms. "You're fucking kidding me, man. Please tell me this is a twisted joke."

"I wish I could. I'd never joke about something so important."

John swore a blue streak as he clenched and unclenched his fists. Finally, he sank onto the couch.

"There's more." *Fuck.* Dread knotted my stomach, making me queasy.

He pinned me with an intense stare. "What could be worse than that fucker walking around and being able to hurt Eva again?"

163

John was right. Eva staying here was worse, but I realized he'd still take it hard.

"Her parents decided to move away. As in, out of state away. They don't feel that Eva can heal while Brandon is on the loose."

The color drained from John's cheeks. Even though he and Eva hadn't had an official date, we all knew he was in love with her.

"I'm so sorry, dude. I'll give you some space. I'm heading to Mac's to tell her about Eva. If you need anything, text me."

"Oh damn. Mac hasn't heard the news yet?" He pulled on the hem of his navy shirt, scrunching the fabric in his hand. I'd known him long enough to recognize that he was attempting to control his temper by the rigid set of his jaw and the slump of his shoulders.

"Nope. Dad is going to call Janice, and I want to be there when Mac finds out. I should be the one to tell her."

"Why don't you have her come over? Call Cade, and we'll help you be there for her. We can order whatever she wants for dinner. I'll even pick up her favorite ice cream. She's going to take it hard. Hell, I'm fucking taking it hard and I've not known Eva as long as she has."

I chewed on John's suggestion, weighing out

the pros and cons of her finding out with all of us there. "I think she's going to need a minute to catch her breath. How about I bring her over after I talk to her? She'll probably want a distraction, too."

"Sounds good. I'll text Cade to tell him to get his ass over here. Do you care if I fill him in?" John's shoulders hunched forward. "This whole thing is such a pile of shit."

"I'm with ya. Go ahead and tell him." I glanced at my watch. "I'll text when I'm on my way back with Mac. While I'm out, I'll pick up some food for all of us, too."

John collected the sheet music off the floor. "Whatever Mac wants, I'm good with."

A beat of silence filled the space between us. "I'm sorry, man. I hate that the little fucker got off scot-free and that Eva is moving."

John wore his heart on his sleeve, and right now, I could hear the sound of it breaking. Nothing I could say would help him feel better either.

"Me too. Thanks for letting me know, Hendrix."

IF I THOUGHT John was difficult to deliver the news to, I was mistaken. I swallowed hard, almost choking on the lump in my throat.

"Hendrix, you need to spit it out now. My brain is racing in a million directions of all the horrible shit that could come out of your mouth. Like did Franklin die? Do you have cancer? Did Mom lose her job, and you offered to tell me? Help me out a little, will ya?" She placed her hands on her hips, her foot tapping impatiently against the carpeted loft of her house. Mac looked adorable in her blue jean overalls, white tank top, and hair in two braids. If the situation hadn't been so grim, I'm not sure I would have been able to take her seriously.

I rubbed my jawline. It was time I quit stalling. I nodded to the oversized grey sofa. "You might want to sit down, Mac."

Janice was in her room talking to Dad, so all of the overwhelming emotions were about to run rampant.

Mac sat on the edge of the couch, her body rigid with tension. She wrung her hands in her lap.

"There won't be any charges against Brandon. Dad didn't get all of the details, but it's over. The

DNA evidence is gone." I held my breath waiting for the news to sink in with her.

She stared at me, her cheeks burning bright red, and she clutched her chest.

"Mac? Are you all right?" I asked. Maybe my words had just sent Mac over the edge.

20

If I thought John shot off the couch with record speed, Mac made him look like he'd moved in slow motion.

Mac gawked at me, speechless. "Oh." A variety of emotions flickered in her eyes—shock, disbelief, and anger. She tilted her chin in the air, defiance written all over her face. "This isn't over for him," she whispered, her voice cracking and betraying her feelings.

"Mac …" I reached for her, but she jerked away.

She grabbed her braided pigtails and tugged on them, and I cringed. "That motherfucker!" She dropped to her knees, her anger and heartbreak doubling her over. Mac fisted her hands as her cries shook her shoulders.

I knelt next to her and wrapped my arms around her. Her nails dug into my back as she bunched up my polo shirt in her fingers. "I'm here," I whispered against her hair.

"How? How could he get away with hurting Eva?" she hiccupped.

"I'm not sure how it played out, Mac. Dad suspects Brandon's father pulled some strings."

"Eva won't want to go to the same college as that sick fuck. She'll be terrified." My heart was in my throat while Mac clung to me as I explained to her that Eva and her family would be moving out of state.

Mac's wail filled the room. As close as the girls were, it would most likely feel as devastating as a breakup. Mac didn't have many female friends, and she preferred a small group. We were the same that way.

"Eva's parents will help her. You're my main concern now, Mac." Although I hadn't intended on telling her about the house, I wanted her to know she always had a safe place to sleep and be herself. Especially after she started classes in a few short months and shared the same college campus as Brandon.

Mac released me and glanced up at me with a

red nose and cheeks. I wiped her tears away with the pad of my thumb. "Can you keep a secret?"

Mac chewed on her bottom lip and nodded.

"I … we put an offer on a house today. If it goes well, I'll have my own place. It has a room for you, too."

She blinked excessively, staring at me in shock. "What? I thought you and Franklin were making headway."

Leaning against the sofa, I stretched my legs in front of me. "We are. We're doing great. We're doing so well it scares me a little."

Mac tucked her legs beneath her and propped her elbow on the edge of the couch, searching me for any telltale signs that I was blowing sunshine up her ass to make her feel better.

"It seems like the last few weeks, ever since … Eva." My voice cracked with sadness. "I was so angry. I thought I was going to lose my shit, Mac. The night Brandon pulled that crap with you … I ran home. If I hadn't, I'd have shown up at his place and beat him into oblivion."

"You should have."

"I promised Dad I'd stay out of it, but that's before Brandon walked away without paying for what he did to Eva, not to mention the other girls we don't even know about yet."

"Hendrix, you still need to stay out of it," Janice said, cutting off mine and Mac's conversation while entering the loft. My attention landed on her. She looked nice in her jeans and lilac-colored blouse. Janice's makeup was impeccable, and her blonde hair flowed past her shoulders. She toyed with the heart-shaped necklace that graced her dainty neck. If Janice had been anyone else's mom, she'd be seriously hot.

Inwardly I grimaced. I'd been so deep in thought I hadn't heard Janice come up the stairs.

"I'll try," I mumbled.

Janice sat on the couch next to Mac and rubbed her daughter's back. "Hi, baby. I want you to remember that Brandon will suffer the consequences of his actions. I'm not sure how or when, but at some point, not even his father will be able to protect him."

Mac glanced up at her mom. "Are you sure? I thought the bad guys always won. Except for Superman, but he's not real so he's not a good example in this situation."

Janice nodded. "I've lived long enough to see people's actions catch up with them. This isn't over, honey. Word will eventually spread that Brandon got away with it, and other girls will come forward." Janice pinned me with an intense gaze. "Promise me, Hendrix. Stay away from Brandon. I don't want you mixed up in any of this."

Nervous silence stretched between us, my mind scrambling for what to say. "I can't make you that promise, Janice. I'm sorry. I will say that I'll do my damnedest, but I can't give you my word. If he comes after Mac again ... or he starts to hurt someone else."

Janice's expression filled with compassion. "You've always been the protector, Hendrix. I love you for that, hon. But don't sacrifice your well-being and future for him. Don't misunderstand me. If Brandon were threatening Mac or another girl, I'd expect you to step in, but don't seek him out. Please."

I detected vulnerability in her tone. "I'm training with Charles." The words flew out of my mouth without permission. "Since Brandon and I boxed together, he'd anticipate my moves. This way, I have a better chance of ..." I rubbed the back of my neck and blew out a sigh. "I won't seek him out."

Janice's shoulders visibly relaxed with my words.

"I won't promise anything else, though." I glanced at Mac while her red-rimmed eyes teared up again. Pausing and weighing my next words, I decided to tell Janice. "I was just telling Mac that I made an offer … Dad put an offer on a house for me. There will be an extra bedroom for Mac. If she feels unsafe at college, she can stay with me. I don't want her walking around scared that she'll run into Brandon."

This time it was Janice who teared up. "Thank you, Hendrix. I have to admit that I feel better about you being on the same campus as Mac. I realize it's only half an hour away from here, but I can't always be with her, as we already know. At least you'll be close."

"Tell us about the house," Mac said, smacking me on the shoulder and perking up.

I couldn't stop the excited grin from spreading across my face. After I explained the multiple offer situation and the upgrades I wanted to do if my offer was accepted, Mac was practically dancing in the middle of the loft.

"Ohmigosh! This is so exciting! You have to let me know as soon as you hear something. What do Cade and John think?" She clapped her hands and bounced on her tiptoes.

"Nothing. I won't tell them unless the sellers accept. I don't want John to think he has to move or stress about it right now."

Mac plunked back down on the floor and propped her elbow on Janice's knee. Mac's mouth formed an enormous 'O'. "Damn, I hadn't thought about that. I was too excited about your first place. And I know that Franklin is buying the place for you, but, dude. That's huge in itself. He's totally trying to make things right. I hope you don't feel guilty or some stupid shit for taking his money. You've always been goal-oriented, but this is about your relationship healing with your dad. Mind you, it's about damned time he stepped it up, but he really is! Right, Mom?" Mac finally took a breath and peeked at Janice.

"He's really trying. It's nice to see. I pray every day it continues, and he's able to make a full comeback." I didn't miss the wistful tone in Janice's voice. Dad's alcoholism had been difficult on everyone.

Suddenly, my stomach growled loudly. Janice and Mac laughed. "John and Cade are waiting for us at the house. Grab your swimsuit along with some clean clothes. You can crash with us tonight."

"Mom? That cool with you?"

"Yeah. I think it would be best if you were surrounded by your friends right now." Janice kissed the top of Mac's head. "I love you both very much. Don't ever forget that."

"You too," I responded while I stood and cracked my back.

"Let me pack some clothes and my toothbrush, then I'll be ready to go, Hendrix." Mac hurried down the hall, leaving Janice and me alone.

Janice rose and folded her arms across her chest. "Franklin loves you, Hendrix."

I stared at her, waiting for her to continue, my heart in my throat.

21

"Franklin hasn't told you about his calls to me, has he?"

Puzzled, I shook my head.

"Sometimes he calls me, asking for some advice on how to reconnect with you." Compassion filled her expression.

My mouth opened and closed, but I was too shocked by what she'd told me. Dad was always a take-charge kind of guy, so the idea that he would talk to Janice floored me.

"Wow! That's some serious shit," Mac said, joining us again. She hefted her overstuffed duffle bag onto her shoulder.

Janice nodded in agreement with her daughter. "It is. The reason I shared that with you, Hendrix, was to let you know that he's doing everything he can to rebuild his relationship with you. With all of us."

"Thanks for telling me. More than that, thanks for helping him. You were hurt too, so I can't imagine it's easy for you."

Janice flashed me a sad smile. "We're all attempting to move forward."

"If he's really trying, then I'll cut him some slack." Mac dropped her bag on the floor with a loud thud, breaking through the seriousness in the room.

"I'll grab that for you. I have no idea how you pack so much for one night."

Mac giggled. "Who said it's for one night? If you're moving out, someone has to keep Franklin company in that big ass house. Might as well be me living in luxury."

Laughter filled the room, then we told Janice goodbye. She could probably use an evening to herself. With the long hours she worked, she deserved a night off to relax.

Mac bounded down the stairs while Janice and I followed her, then the doorbell rang.

"I've got it," Janice said, but Mac hadn't heard her.

Without even checking who it was, Mac flung

the door open.

"Dammit," Janice mumbled, side-stepping me to reach her daughter.

"Who are you?" Mac blurted.

"Mac," Janice gently chided. "It's for me."

Finally glimpsing who Mac was talking to, I was unable to contain my surprise. I didn't know many of Janice's friends, but this guy was dressed well. Like, out for dinner on a date kind of nice. I cleared my throat and approached the group.

"I'm Timothy." He gave Mac a wide smile. "I'm here for your mom."

A bright pink dusted Janice's cheeks.

Mac whirled around, noticing her mom's embarrassment. "Your boyfriend?"

"Sorry, Tim. My daughter was leaving. Have fun, honey." Janice kissed Mac on the forehead, then gave me a quick hug as she nearly pushed us out the front door.

I glanced over my shoulder as Janice let Timothy inside.

"Holy shit balls. Mom has a date!" Mac stared at me dumbfounded.

"Shh. Get in the car, then we can talk." I grinned at her. It was nice to see Janice having a social life. I suspected she had one and we just didn't know about it. Janice had always been a private person.

Mac and I climbed into my Camry, and I started the engine.

"Mom's gonna get laid!" Mac's hands flew over her mouth and she giggled. "Hell, she needs to. Work some of that stress out."

I couldn't help but laugh as I backed out of the driveway. "Speaking of stress, what do you want to pick up for dinner on the way home?"

That did the trick. Mac loved food, and it immediately took her mind in a different direction. Once Mac had decided on sushi, thoughts of Andrea drifted through my mind. I was still in shock that I'd asked her out. I'd almost told Mac about her, but after her reaction with Janice and Timothy, I chose to keep my mouth shut. We'd see how the date went first.

The rest of the evening was filled with conversation about Eva and Brandon. Cade and John stuck close to Mac, giving her the extra affection she craved. It would be hardest for Mac to adjust. With her ADHD, a change could present a huge challenge for her. At the root of her struggle, though, was the fear that she'd never have a best friend like Eva again. Mac had gone through some difficult years in middle and high school.

She'd been called a weirdo and made fun of. I'd tried to stave off as much of the bullshit as I could, but I wasn't with Mac all of the time. I hoped like hell I wouldn't fail her with Brandon. No matter the cost, I had to make sure she was safe.

2 2

$\mathcal{C}$harles eased the Mercedes into Andrea's driveway a few minutes early. He'd offered to ring her doorbell and walk her to the car, but I'd turned him down. The last thing I needed was to scare the poor girl. Charles hadn't mastered a warm and friendly demeanor yet. Plus, I hadn't mentioned a bodyguard to her because I hadn't planned on bringing him, but Dad had insisted.

A soft breeze kicked up as I climbed out of the backseat of the vehicle. I'd selected a blue-and-white striped button-down tucked into my Kiton straight-legged jeans. Instead of my Nikes or Converse, I'd stepped into black Stefano Ricci slip-ons. I applied a light spritz of Clive Christian

X Spray before I left Dad's. The combination of vanilla, cinnamon, and cedarwood had always been a favorite of mine. Maybe it would be one of Andrea's too.

I approached the white ranch-style house as the familiar smell of summer lingered in the air. Rows of magnolias and chrysanthemums added a colorful touch to the front of the home. The black window shutters matched the flower boxes, and the soft buzz of a bee caught my attention. The lawn was freshly mowed and well taken care of too. Andrea's family obviously took pride in their place.

I sucked in a deep breath and swallowed my nerves. Wiping my clammy hands on my jeans, I rang the doorbell. It'd been a long time since I'd been nervous about a date, but I didn't go out often.

The door opened, and a tall dark-haired woman in her late forties answered. She wore light blue scrubs, and I wondered if she was a nurse. "You must be Hendrix. I'm Andrea's mother. Please, come in." She moved back and offered me a warm smile.

"Thank you." I entered the tan tile entryway and extended my hand to Andrea's mom. "It's nice to meet you."

"Call me Patricia. Andrea will be ready in a minute." She eyed me appreciatively. "Andrea said that you're the lead singer of August Clover."

"I am." I smiled at her, hoping she didn't think I was a drug-and-women-addicted rock star. I quickly scanned the comfortable living room. An oversized brown leather couch hugged the wall, and a small woodstove took up the corner. The long coffee table held several books and the television remote. The space was clean and gave off a friendly, homey vibe.

"She played some of your music. You've got an amazing voice. Are you recording another album?" Patricia tucked her hand in the front pocket of her shirt.

It was clear that Andrea had talked about me in relation to being a member of an up-and-coming band, but I couldn't help but wonder if she saw me as Hendrix the person or Hendrix, the lead singer of August Clover.

"Hey," Andrea said, joining us and beaming at me.

Apparently we were on the same wavelength because Andrea wore an emerald green blouse tucked into her dark wash jeans. The polish on her nails and toes matched her shirt, too. She looked really nice.

"Hey." I returned her smile. "Are you ready? I made reservations so we wouldn't have to wait to be seated."

"Oh, where are you going?" Patricia asked.

I glanced at Andrea. "Clinkendaggers. We have a table outside. Is that okay?"

"Yes! That sounds perfect," Andrea replied enthusiastically, tossing her long brown hair over a shoulder. "I've only been there a few times. The food is so good! The ambiance and scenery are amazing, too. I almost forget about the river until I slow down long enough to spend some time near it." Andrea laughed.

Relieved that she liked the restaurant I'd picked for us, I grinned at her. "The weather is perfect as well." I gave her mom a small wave goodbye. "It was nice to meet you, Patricia."

"You kids have fun."

I allowed Andrea to walk in front of me as we stepped outside, my attention landing on her firm ass and the soft sway of her hips. Her jeans fit her even better from this view.

"Holy crap," Andrea whispered, breaking my train of thought.

Inwardly I groaned. She'd spotted Charles, who was standing near the Mercedes with the back door open.

"Uh. Sorry. I have security tonight. Try to ignore him."

"Seriously?" Her pitch rose slightly.

I stopped walking. "Is it a problem?" I asked gently. This is why I hadn't wanted Charles with me tonight, I had no idea how Andrea would react, but Dad had put his foot down. Maybe he'd received an update from the FBI. I wasn't sure, but he was in full-on protective mode before I left the house.

"No. I'm sorry. It just took me off guard." She placed her hand on my arm. "You're a lead singer for a popular band, it makes sense."

"I'm not used to it yet," I confessed, a hint of irritation in my tone.

We slipped into the backseat, then Charles returned to the driver's side. He'd left the car running and music was playing quietly in the background. I nearly laughed as I recognized the song by Jeffrey James, "All I Need is You." Charles was setting the mood.

Andrea and I kept the topics light as he drove us to the restaurant. Relief flooded me when we were seated, and Charles stood at the other end of the outdoor patio.

"Oh, man." I rubbed the back of my neck and leaned back in the iron chairs. "It's difficult to have a conversation with him around." A chuckle rumbled through my chest.

"He's very … serious." She pursed her lips together as she eyed him.

"That he is."

Andrea turned toward the rushing sound of the Spokane River and took a deep breath. "I don't eat here often, but it's so beautiful out here."

I appreciated that she hadn't brought up the cost of the restaurant. I'd drop over a hundred on our meal. The point was to do something different and nice for her. "I thought it might be a good choice since we'd talked about having classes outside." I cracked a grin. "This beats the hell out of Biology."

"Right? And hopefully no one will nearly die, either." An exasperated look crossed her heart-shaped face.

I shook my head, still in disbelief that Professor Kline had dropped to the ground. "You were so calm, but I suspect it messed you up a little. Have you heard how the professor is doing?"

"It did. I just kept reminding myself to breathe and think through my steps. No, I've not talked to the professor. I do know that he won't be teaching class tomorrow. His TA will."

"That makes sense. Hopefully he's feeling better."

The waiter approached our table, interrupting our conversation. I was pleasantly surprised when Andrea ordered a steak. Other girls I'd taken out barely ate. There were times I struggled not to let it bother me when they took two bites of a sixty-dollar meal, then refused to take home the leftovers. Even if they threw it away as soon as they walked into their house, it would have been nice if they'd appeased me a little.

Andrea squinted at me, the sun directly in her eyes. I scooted around the table, pulling her closer to me. "Is that better?"

"Much. I'd prefer to see you when we're talking." She smiled and draped her arm on the back of her chair.

Over the next two hours, we discussed politics, religion, and other unacceptable topics for a first date. She was respectful in her opinions and had no problem when I disagreed with her. In fact, she challenged my thought process. It was some of the most stimulating conversation I'd ever had, and I loved it. Andrea was highly intelligent and comfortable in her own skin, not to mention pretty.

My phone buzzed against the iron tabletop,

and I flipped it over. "It's my alarm. I need to get to the studio."

"How often do you book it?" Andrea asked, standing.

"Every chance we get. At least twice a week when we're recording." I tapped the hard case on my cell, then placed my palm in the middle of Andrea's back. Without any hesitation, she closed the gap between us. I understood the cue and took her hand in mine, our fingers intertwining. "I'm sorry I have to end the date early."

"I understand." She grabbed her to-go box. "I love leftovers." She scrunched her nose at me and giggled. "Maybe I'm weird, but it will make a great study snack."

We continued to talk on the way back to her place. Once there, I walked her to the door. My pulse kicked up a notch as I pondered whether to kiss her or not. "I had a nice time. I'll see you tomorrow in class?"

Andrea glanced up at me. "Thank you for dinner, and yes. I'll be there."

An awkward silence filled the space between us. "Can I kiss you?" I asked. Assuming was never a good idea, so I always asked a girl the first time.

"Please." Her voice was soft and breathy.

Leaning down, I gently pressed my lips

against hers. She wrapped her arms around my neck and drew me closer. Andrea's mouth melted into mine and a soft moan escaped her as her hot tongue swept across mine. This girl definitely wasn't shy.

I took a step back and tucked a piece of hair behind her ear. "Have a good night and I'll talk to you tomorrow."

"Yeah, that would be great. And thank you again." Pink dusted her cheeks, and she gave me a small wave.

I offered her a genuine smile, then headed back to the car. *Dammit.* That wasn't what I'd expected at all. I'd had a nice afternoon with her, but the moment her lips met mine … nothing. Not a fucking thing. My limp dick even confirmed my suspicions.

The ride to the college seemed like it took years rather than twenty minutes. I needed to talk to Cade and John as soon as I saw them.

23

"**W**hat are you all dressed up for?" Cade asked as I strolled into the studio.

"I had a date." I plunked down in my usual seat at the console, my mood plummeting even more than it had on the ride here. "I think I'm fucking broken."

John chuckled and flipped a lock of his hair out of his eyes. "You're just figuring that out now?"

I dropped my hands into my lap and blew out a noisy sigh. "Not fucking funny."

"What do you mean, and who is she?" Cade asked, sitting in the chair next to me. Eagerness filled his expression while he stared at me, waiting for answers.

"Her name is Andrea Wallace. She's pretty, super smart, and confident. She's a fantastic conversationalist, too. Hell, she even saved Professor Kline's life yesterday."

"Oh. I heard about that." Cade patted his chest with his hand. "That's a good type of person to be friends with, so I started asking around to find out who she is. A guy pointed her out to me. She's fucking hot." Cade punched me in the shoulder. "And you're not fucking her right now? Like, what's the problem, dude?"

"Do you ever think with your brain and not your dick?" I didn't even try to hide the irritation in my tone.

Dismayed, John shot him a look and shook his head. "If you actually like someone, Cade, you don't screw her on the first date."

Cade laughed us off. "So why are you broken, then? I mean if you're not inside her right now, what gives?" An ornery grin pulled at the corner of his mouth.

"I kissed her goodbye, and I didn't feel a damn thing. Nothing. Zip. No chemistry, no attraction … not a fucking thing." I groaned and ran my fingers through my hair. Hell, my cock hadn't even twitched, but I wasn't going to tell the guys that.

"Sometimes it's just not there. No reason to beat yourself up over it," John said while he flipped a drumstick in the air and caught it.

"What if after the messed-up shit I've gone through and seen with Dad, I'm not capable of emotionally connecting with someone? What if … what if Ken—" My breath hitched in my throat. I tossed my hands up in surrender, then hung my head, my hair cloaking my face. I couldn't say her name. The pain was still too intense, threatening to rip my heart out of my chest and never give it back. A part of me realized that falling in love wasn't worth the risk to me. I'd had enough hell and disappointment in my twenty years without extending an invitation for more. I attempted to clear away the agonizing past that was haunting me.

Cade and John stared at me like I'd just announced the Four Horsemen of the Apocalypse had arrived and the world was about to end.

"Is that what you think, man?" Cade grew serious, finally putting the joking aside.

Cade scooted to the edge of his seat, his intense gaze connecting with mine. "What happened wasn't your fault. You did the best that you could. Dude, you were only thirteen. You had the world on your shoulders and way too much responsibility weighing on you."

Tears stung my eyes, and I immediately shifted my attention to my feet. Cade could be a jerk sometimes, but when I needed him, he was always there. Cade knew all about taking care of a family at a young age, too. It was one of the things we'd bonded over so quickly, and I had a lot of respect for him in that area.

"You're not broken, Hendrix," John said quietly. "Out of all of us you have the best moral compass. You won't even take advantage of an opportunity to get laid. From the way it sounds, Andrea is into you, but you chose to walk away and do the right thing by her." John folded his arms across his chest, his drumsticks still in his hands. "There have been plenty of times I didn't."

"I don't feel anything for her. She's fun to talk to, but that's it. I kept waiting to get excited about another date with her, but it never happened. When I arrived at her house to pick her up, I was nervous, but that was all."

John leaned against the studio console and crossed his ankles, the legs of his jeans rustling.

"Don't take it so seriously. Honestly, I think you're the kind of guy that waits for *the one*. You'd rather focus on a career and take your time. There's nothing wrong with that. The way the band is taking off, hell it's smart. You don't want some girl coming after you and spreading lies and shit."

Cade tilted his head at John. "What he said. And I bet the moment you see her you'll know. You'll be a fucking goner." Cade smacked my leg. "Dude, don't stress. Tell Andrea you need to focus on the band, then send her my way." Cade released a low chuckle.

I rolled my eyes at him. "I'd laugh, but I realize that you're not joking."

"As far as the other stuff with your dad goes … I think you're cautious about who you spend your time with. There's nothing wrong with that. Besides, I think the right girl for you will show up when you least expect it." John grinned, agreeing with Cade.

Maybe they were right, and my life experience and choices weren't wrong for me. "I'll talk to her tomorrow after class. I hope she's cool about it and not the type that will be nice to my face and vindictive behind my back. She doesn't seem like she is, but I don't know her very well."

My phone buzzed in my back pocket, and I leaned forward to remove it. My stomach flip-flopped. It was Gabrielle.

"Hi, Gabrielle," I answered, my heart hammering wildly against my chest. I listened intently, then shot out of my chair with a loud whoop. "I got it? Yes! This is amazing. Thank you so much for your help. Have you told Dad yet?"

I caught John and Cade's puzzled expressions. "I'll call him. Yeah. I'm at the studio at the college. Swing on by if you want to. Otherwise, we can do it in the morning. But I think the faster the papers are signed, the better I'll feel." I looked up at the large clock that hung on the wall over the door. "We still have a few hours here, so I'll see you in a little while. Awesome, bye." I disconnected the call and spun around, grinning as though I'd just won the lottery. To me, I had.

"What the hell, man?" John asked, chuckling.

"Hang on." I pulled up Dad's number on my cell, then put it on speaker.

"Hey, son. How are you?"

"Dad!" I couldn't contain my excitement. "They accepted the offer. I got the house!" I glanced at Cade and John as their mouths dropped open.

"Congratulations! That's fantastic news. When

do you sign the papers?" The squeak of Dad's chair told me he was in his office. "I'll need to write the check as well."

"Dude! He bought you your own bachelor pad?" Cade whispered and smacked me on the arm.

I nodded. "Gabrielle is on her way over to the studio. I guess I better get some things done before she gets here. I just wanted to let you know and ..." A ball of gratitude lodged itself in my throat and I struggled to speak. "Thanks, Dad," I said softly. "Thank you for being there for me."

The line grew quiet, and for a fleeting second, I wished John and Cade weren't around. I hadn't expected myself to get so emotional about Dad supporting me.

"Thank you for letting me, son." Dad's voice was tight, and I knew this was a big moment for him as well. "I'll see you tonight when you get home."

"All right. Later." I disconnected the call, then fielded John and Cade's questions.

Before John could ask, I wanted to put his mind at ease. "You don't have to move, John. When we put the offer on the house, Dad said you can stay as long as you need to. I think he'll appreciate the company, honestly."

John shoved his hand in the front pocket of his jeans, unable to hide his sheepish expression from us. "Yeah, about that."

24

"*I* talked to Eva today. She asked if I would help her family move to Montana and stay with them for the summer."

"No shit? What did you say?" That was huge. Even though Eva's parents would be around, it was a chance for her and John to reconnect in a way that felt safe for her.

"I told her I needed to talk to you guys first. Since we have gigs booked for months, and it's my income, I wanted to think about it." Sincerity shadowed John's features. He'd always been loyal to August Clover and to me.

"Are you concerned about finances or a temporary drummer?" Cade asked.

"Both. I have a possible replacement though."

John ran his hand through his hair. "I'm not sure about the money, though. She said she loves me, and wants to take things really slow."

"Wow. That's huge." Cade rubbed his stubbled chin. "So you'll be gone for the summer huh?"

John gave a half shrug. "I'm not sure I can make it work yet, but I wanted to talk to you guys about it."

"Fuck that." I hopped out of my chair. "If you want to be with her, then go. I'll loan you the money, and when you're home again, pay me back a little each gig. You've been in love with her for a long time. You need to see if this can work."

John opened his mouth, then closed it again.

"I'll help, too. I've got money saved. Besides, if you don't go, you're going to be whining like a little bitch for months. I can't hang with that, man." Cade snickered.

John grabbed a pen off the console and chucked it at Cade's head. "Thanks, asshole." John laughed. "A part of me wants to stay. The other part wants to go. If I don't, I think I'll wonder if we would have worked or not. At least if I'm with her for a few months, I'll know for sure one way or the other. I won't have it haunting me the rest of my life."

"I'd do the same. You'll have a place to come

back to. Dad's cool with you staying there if you want to. Plus, I have a three-bedroom house I'm about to buy. You can stay with me when you come back, too."

"Are you sure?" Hesitation hung on John's question. "You guys are really okay if I go?"

I glanced at Cade, then at John. "I'm in. For all the times you've been there for me, this is the least I can do. We're brothers."

Cade remained quiet for a beat. "I think it says a lot that Eva wants to spend time together. After what she went through, it sounds like she's serious about you. And I agree. If you don't go, you'll have that question running around in your head for the rest of your life." Cade averted our gazes and stared at his shoes. "Don't let her be the one that got away. Trust me on this, it fucking sucks." Cade cleared his throat and turned away from us.

What the fuck just happened? Cade had never talked about a girl seriously. Whoever it was still had his heart, which explained why he was such a man whore. I suspected he was trying to fill the void with other women.

John nodded at our friend, questions written all over his face. I shook my head. Maybe over the summer I'd learn more about who she was, but

Cade had been silent about her for this long, and I wasn't sure he'd budge.

"If you're sure, I'll go. I'd do the same for either of you guys too," John said. "I can hop on FaceTime with you for our jamming sessions. Eva's parents said they won't be out in the boonies, so they'll have reliable internet."

"That sounds good. We'll work it out, man. Don't sweat it." I gently slapped him on the back. We were recording our last song this week anyway, so we didn't need the studio time for a while. "Besides, Montana is only a four-to-six-hour drive depending on where you'll be. We can visit if we need to." I grinned.

"Get the hell out of here and be with Eva and her family. Help her get better." Cade laced his fingers behind his head and pursed his lips. "It won't be the same without you, dude. Hendrix will have to entertain me when you're gone." Cade glanced at me as the corner of his mouth kicked up in a grin.

"When do you leave?" I asked, realizing how much I was going to miss John.

"In two days. I think it will be good for me." John rubbed his chin, a puzzled expression settling in. "I was shocked to hear from Eva, not to mention that she wanted me to spend the summer there."

"I'd take that as a great sign. Maybe she's trying to move forward. Are you going to tell Mac?" I asked while dread twisted my stomach into knots. This would fucking crush Mac, and she'd been through enough already.

Sadness flashed across John's expression. His attention dropped to the floor, then back to Cade and me. "Eva doesn't want to talk to her right now. I know it's not right or fair to Mac, but Eva feels like ... Eva feels like if Mac had been watching out for her the assault wouldn't have happened."

Cade released a low whistle. "You're kidding, right?" Cade asked before I had time to open my mouth.

"I'm sorry. That's where Eva's head is right now. I'll see if I can talk to her over the summer, but I don't want to push her to reach out to Mac. I think Eva's too raw and angry to think clearly. I'm not sure how to help her understand that Mac was the one that stopped the assault. She's not realized you two saved her from a potentially worse situation. I don't think she can process it yet."

"That's bullshit." I folded my arms across my chest. Every cell in my body burned with a desire to protect Mac. "It wasn't Mac's fault." Anger infiltrated my veins and slithered into every part of me. "Has it even occurred to Eva that she could have been a victim of gang rape if Mac hadn't shown up?" I turned away and stared into the empty recording booth, attempting to regain my composure. There wasn't a damned thing about this situation that was easy or fair. Eva had been raped, and Mac was the one paying for it. Grinding my molars, I imagined pummeling Brandon's smug face to a bloody pulp. He should have never been able to walk away without any consequences.

John nodded. "I know, but Eva can't handle thinking about the what ifs. She's angry and Mac's the easiest person to blame. I hope she'll come around after she has some time to heal."

I dropped my hands. "Don't get me wrong, I like Eva, but she was passed out while Mac was guarding her. In no way am I blaming Eva. All I'm trying to explain is that unless Eva talks to Mac, she has no idea how much her best friend took care of her. Eva's clothes were off, and she was completely vulnerable. Mac did everything she could, including hitting Brandon over the head with a fucking hockey stick." My irritation was quickly escalating.

"What he said." Cade nodded at me. "Eva needs to know the truth, man."

"What am I supposed to do, though?" John rocked back and forth on his heels, worry lines creasing his forehead. "I want to listen and support how she feels. At the same time, Mac is family. I'm torn."

I blew out a big breath. It wasn't fair to put all of the responsibility on John's shoulders. "Do the best you can. It's all you can do. Just see how it goes. The last thing we want is for Eva to shut down again."

"She barely started talking to me about the party. It's going to be a day at a time, ya know?" John said.

"Well, we have some recording to do before Gabrielle gets here. After the studio session I'll drive you guys by the house tonight if you want." The thought of myself as a homeowner immediately lifted my mood.

Cade sang a few lines of our new song, and I grinned at him. He'd been on backup vocals since we'd formed the band, but eventually he'd take the spotlight. He was too damned good not to.

THE REST OF THE NIGHT, I walked around Dad's place with a big ass smile on my face. All of the papers had been signed, and I'd take possession of the home in three weeks, which also allowed time for an inspection. Dad had insisted on hiring a company to move me. At first, I objected. I had Cade, Dad, Charles, and Mac to help. Eventually I stopped arguing with him. I wasn't going to win this one.

As soon as I had the keys, I'd show Mac and Cade the inside of the house. Since John would be in Montana, I'd have to FaceTime him. Mac was deliriously happy and excited to see her room. I had a feeling she'd be at my place a lot over the summer, and I was okay with that. My news also helped soften the blow about Eva leaving.

I hadn't been able to tell her that Eva blamed Mac for Brandon's attack. The words refused to form on my tongue, so I had to trust it wasn't the right time. Surely Eva would move through the anger and not blame anyone except the sorry son of a bitch who had hurt her. Brandon was a disgusting piece of shit, and ever since I'd known him in middle school when he wanted something, he took it, but it hadn't ever been a girl. I assumed he'd grow out of the behavior, but he hadn't. What puzzled me the most was the change in him. We'd never been best friends, but we'd hung out some, especially while we were boxing. So what the hell happened?

It was almost one in the morning when I crawled into bed, exhausted but content. I'd met Charles in the gym for another self-defense lesson and sparring. He didn't talk a lot, but he certainly was helping me feel more confident in my abilities to hammer Brandon into the ground if I needed to. Maybe he'd leave Mac alone now that the charges had been dropped. If he knew what was good for him, he would. If not, I'd be ready for him.

25

Two days later, I dragged my feet down the hill, kicking at the tiny pebbles along the way to the guesthouse. I'd offered to help John pack his belongings, but he didn't have much. He was a basic needs kind of guy. Now that the band was taking off, he had more financial freedom, and I wondered if he'd branch out with some fun purchases like a new car.

I stood in front of the door, sadness swirling around in the pit of my stomach. Even though it was only for three months, I was going to miss John more than I wanted to admit. It didn't matter that I was moving; he would still have been at my place all the time. But now he'd be living in another state. My throat clogged up, loneliness beckoning to me with her long, bony finger. She and I had been friends for too many years, and it was easy for me to slip back into the black hole I'd dug my way out of while I lived with Mac and Janice. The little voice in my head reminded me Cade wasn't leaving and neither was Mac, but they weren't John. Each person had a special place in my life, and although I hadn't expressed my concern, I was worried John wouldn't come back.

Sucking up my emotions, I squared my shoulder and lifted my chin. John needed my support, not my self-pity. I swung the door open and poked my head into the entryway. "Hey!" I called out.

John had his back to me, his hands on his hips as his attention traveled over his belongings that were strown all over the living room floor.

"Need help packing?" I offered, stifling a laugh. "Dude, no offense, but this is worse than what I'd expect from a girl. Are you planning on coming back?"

John narrowed his eyes at me. "Not funny, man. Of course I'm coming back, but I have no idea what Montana is like during the summer. Are the nights cold? If so, I need jeans and a hoodie. And how cold? Do I need boots to walk the property or will my leather tennis shoes work?"

No longer able to hold my laughter in, I lost it. "All right. Hang on a minute." I removed my phone from my back pocket and pulled up the weather app. "What city will you be in?"

"Kalispell." He plopped down on the couch. "This is harder than I thought it'd be. I definitely want to be with her, that's not what I mean. I'm well aware that she's trying to heal from her trauma, and I have no idea what to expect."

Tapping my screen, I brought up the weather app and entered the city for him. "It's cooler than it is here." I handed my phone to him. "As far as Eva, try to give her as much love and support as you can. Don't rush anything and listen when she needs to talk. Don't try to convince her that she shouldn't feel a certain way, either. You consistently showing up for her is all she needs right now."

John frowned. "How do you know all of that?" He handed my cell back to me.

"Because it's what I needed after …" There wasn't any need to remind John of what had happened. He'd seen my soul shatter into a million pieces, then watched as I slowly stitched it together again. Dwelling on the past certainly didn't help me either. Feeling like shit was no longer on my agenda. Dad and I were healing, I was in a good place in my life, and that's what I wanted to focus on.

"It's solid advice. I'm sure I'll text a lot," John said.

"I'm here any time you need me."

Over the next few hours, we packed and cleaned. It would be strange to not see John every day or hang out with him in the guesthouse. The mere thought of it tugged on my heartstrings, but he deserved this time with Eva. Both of them needed to see if they wanted to pursue a serious relationship, and I hoped it worked out. All I wanted was for my friends to be happy.

"Hey, did you call Jacob yet?" John asked.

"No, but if you're recommending him as our drummer for the summer, I'm sure he'll be fine. Not you, but good." I cracked a grin at him. "I'll call him later."

"He's pretty excited to play with August Clover." John chuckled. "It's still weird to be a part of a band that people love."

"Yeah, it is, but it's fun." Never in my wildest dreams had I thought August Clover would have come this far. The potential we had was huge, and I was eager to see the possibilities.

John and I continued with the small talk until five o'clock rolled around, and it was time for him to leave. He drove his car down the hill, and we loaded his belongings into the trunk and backseat.

"I'll send you pictures of my new house, and if you need a place to stay when you get back, you have a room there or here." Goodbyes sucked ass even if it was for a little while.

"Thanks, man." John gave me a hug. "Wish me luck."

"You don't need it. You've got this." I patted him on the back, then stepped away.

John gave me a small wave, sadness clinging to his expression. I wondered if he was having second thoughts, but I wouldn't be the one to bring it up. Plus I didn't want to look like an asshole if I was wrong.

I stood in the driveway and watched John begin the ascent up the hill, his Honda's red taillights blinking at me. Defected, I folded my arms across my chest and reminded myself of all the things that were going well in my life. John deserved the same, and three months would pass quickly.

My phone buzzed and Cade's name popped up on my screen.

I've got a night off, let's find some trouble to get into.

Part of me wanted to immediately refuse, but Cade rarely had a chance to go out.

I'm not interested in finding someone to hook up with.

Little black dots flickered across the screen.

Shit, I forgot to ask how it went with Andrea. Did you talk to her yesterday? How did she take the news?

I rubbed the back of my neck with my free hand, recalling the disappointment on her face when I explained I needed to focus on my career.

She said she understood, but we'll see if she gives me the cold shoulder.

I shielded my eyes from the golden late afternoon sun and began walking to Dad's house.

Do you want to invite Mac? Maybe she'd like to have a few drinks and dance or shoot pool or whatever we decide to do. I know everything with Eva has been hard.

It wasn't unusual for Cade or John to want to include Mac, but I still questioned his intentions with her. It didn't matter anyway. She was working at the pizzeria tonight. It was the perfect job for her since she brought leftover pizza home every night. I wondered if she'd eventually get sick of it.

She has plans tonight, so it's just us. Are we getting an Uber? If so, why don't you crash here if you can.

Once we'd agreed on an Uber and plans, I opened the door leading into the kitchen. Dad wouldn't care if Cade slept here, but I wanted to let him know. We'd have to be quiet when we came in later. My goal was to avoid Dad while we smelled like alcohol.

I strolled through the house and headed to Dad's office. His deep voice carried down the hallway. I didn't miss the hushed tone either. Taking great care not to make any noise, I decided to eavesdrop.

"Gabby, I'd love to take you out for dinner," Dad said. His tone was low and soothing.

The world paused around me, and I nearly groaned. What if Gabby became my stepmother? My stomach churned at the thought of her and Dad sharing a bedroom. My nostrils flared in disgust. I realized my Dad had a right to have an active and healthy sex life, but it didn't mean I wanted to think about it. Gabrielle was nice, but it grossed me out the way she threw herself at Dad.

I'd already heard enough. I spun around and ran into a solid wall of muscle. "Fuck, Charles. Seriously?" I glared at him.

Charles's gaze narrowed briefly. "I was about to ask you the same thing."

I tossed my hands up in front of me. "I'm out of here. I overheard enough."

Charles chuckled and I gawked at him. After I was able to scoop my mouth off the floor, I recovered.

"You laugh." It wasn't a question.

"Of course I do. I'm human." Charles's stoic expression had already slipped back into place.

I waited for him to move out of my way, but he remained in the middle of the hallway. "Is there something I can do for you?" Charles catching me listening to Dad's conversation wasn't settling well with me.

"No. I'm waiting to speak with your father when he's off the phone." He nodded in the direction of Dad's office. "But from the end of the hall where I can't hear his conversation." He smirked at me.

"Until you stood behind me." I clenched my jaw together. "You probably heard everything I did." I cocked a brow at him. If he was going to be a condescending ass, I'd give it right back to him. "I was going to tell Dad I'm going out with Cade tonight, but since he's occupied, I'll find him later."

"I'll see if your father has plans. If not, I'll drive you."

A sinking feeling nudged me with a sharp elbow. Folding my arms across my chest, I stared at him. I wasn't backing down from my decision. "It won't be necessary. We're calling an Uber and we'll be out late. We need to have some fun and blow off some steam, so having a bodyguard with me won't work."

Charles didn't respond. In fact, if he'd not been standing in front of me, I'd wondered if he'd heard what I'd said. "I'm headed upstairs, so if you'll excuse me." Irritation tugged at me. Sometimes Charles was a bit much to take.

Instead of arguing with me, Charles moved out of my way.

"Have a good evening." He nodded in my direction.

Suspicious, I walked past him, then ran up the stairs to my bedroom. Even I knew that Charles was up to something. Pushing the thought out of my mind, I decided I was going to have a good time. Cade had the right idea. It was time to blow off some steam and have fun.

I couldn't wait until I moved into my new place and Charles wouldn't be in my face. If Dad and Gabrielle started dating, they'd need their space too. Ugh. I wanted Dad happy, but not with her.

After I chose my jeans and shirt for the evening, I headed to the shower. As hard as I tried, I couldn't shake the uneasiness that shadowed me as I showered and dressed. Little did I know how much the events of that night would change my life forever.

26

Jimmy Z's Gastropub & Red Room Lounge was packed to the brim. The line to the bar was nearly impossible to squeeze through, and the dance floor was overflowing with gyrating bodies. I wasn't familiar with the band, but they sounded good as they sang a cover of "Love on the Brain" by Rihanna.

Spokane was definitely on the light side for clubs, but August Clover had performed here several times, so we were friends with the manager, Bobby Daily. The red décor was bold, and the woodwork was stunning. It fit the high-energy vibe. Out of all the detailed interior, my favorite feature was the bar that reached to the ceiling.

"We should have planned ahead and asked Dad if we could have taken his plane to Seattle and returned in the morning." I smoothed my navy polo shirt that I'd tucked into my straight-fit jeans.

"No shit. It was a spur of the moment night off from taking care of the family, so I'm grateful to be out." Cade yelled over the music at me. "What do you want to drink? I'll get the first round." Cade's eyes twinkled with mischief.

I pondered for a minute. We had an Uber, and worst-case scenario, we'd call Charles for a ride home. My goal for the night was to relax and have fun.

"Long Island," I roared over the deafening noise of the club. I reached for my wallet in my back pocket, but Cade shook his head, then began moving in the direction of the bar.

Wondering if he'd remember to tip well, I scanned the area for a seat. Not finding any, I moved over to a corner of the room that was less crowded. Cade would still be able to spot me, but I wanted to have a drink before I asked anyone to dance.

A few minutes later, Cade worked his way through the crowd and approached the little round two-top table I was standing next to.

"Here ya go." Cade handed the Long Island to me.

"That was fast!" I yelled over the deafening noise of the music.

"Yeah, Bobby saw me, so we got served pretty quick. I'm enjoying the perks of being a member of August Clover." Cade grinned and downed a few shots.

Suddenly the music stopped, and I spotted Bobby walking out on stage. "Thanks to everyone for coming down tonight!"

Cheers and clapping filled the room.

"While Jim and the band take a break, I'd like to welcome Hendrix Harrington and Cade Richardson from August Clover. Come on up and play, guys." He waved us toward the front of the bar.

Cade bumped me with his elbow and grinned as though he knew all along that Bobby was going to invite us up. "Come on, man."

"Dude, John's gone. We don't have a drummer." Chants for August Clover reached my ears, and I inwardly groaned. I hadn't planned on singing tonight, but it was free press.

As soon as I was about to decline, the drummer from the earlier band sauntered on stage and sat down at the drum set.

I shot Cade a suspicious look. "Guess you have it all covered, huh?"

"Yup. If we want to stay booked here, we've gotta give them something to come back for." Cade set his empty shot glasses on the table next to us. He rolled his shoulders, then cracked his neck. Without another word, he pushed me in front of him. "Look at all of the girls, man. In a song or two, they'll be lining up and hoping to scream your name later." Cade offered me a lop-sided grin.

I shook my head. Cade was always thinking about getting laid.

The chanting grew louder, and I knew Cade was right. As soon as I began to walk to the stage, the crowd parted for us. Squeals from the ladies reached my ears, and I chuckled. Unlike Cade, I wasn't sure I'd ever get used to the fans.

Hopping on stage, I smiled at the sea of people as Bobby handed Cade a guitar. Cade played a few chords, then broke out into a crazy good riff. He was born to perform.

The entire place went wild as he finished. I mouthed a song name to the drummer, and he nodded, then counted down for us. Since I hadn't prepared anything, I fell back on one of my favorite songs, "Could You Be Mine?" by Billy Raffoul. My tenor voice floated through the speakers as my mind disappeared into the lyrics. The longer we sang, the louder the girls screamed. Before I realized it, the only people left on the dance floor were women.

I glanced at Cade, who had a huge grin plastered on his face. Next, we played "Tempt My Trouble" by Bishop Briggs. Once we finished, I thanked Bobby and everyone for allowing us to play. I strolled over to the drummer and shook his hand. He was good, and maybe he'd be a perfect backup if we ever needed one. I mentally kicked myself for thinking that way. John would be back in a few months. I hoped.

Cade and I exited the stage and were greeted by several girls. One blonde in particular caught my eye. Her jeans were tucked into her black boots, and her red shirt dipped low enough to show a nice amount of cleavage. My gaze connected with hers, and I smiled while I approached her.

"You're amazing," she said, offering me a shy smile.

"Thanks." I ran my fingers through my hair. "I'm glad you liked it." A deep bass shook the speakers, then "The Devil You Know" by X-Ambassadors began to play. "Do you want to dance?"

"I'd love to. I'm Josie, by the way."

"Nice to meet you. I'm Hendrix."

She giggled. "I know." Josie took my hand and led me to the dance floor. We found a small space near the center of the room, then Josie started to dance. She slipped one long leg between mine and practically humped my leg. She pressed her big tits against my chest and placed her hand on my stomach. *Holy shit, so much for thinking she was shy.*

My cock twitched. Damn, it had been a long time since I'd gotten laid.

Josie continued to dance, and before I realized it, she'd placed my palm on her slender ass. I quickly moved it to her lower back.

"Have you been here for a while?" I wondered if she was drunk.

"Yeah, a few hours. Long enough to get plastered. We were about to leave right before you arrived."

She tugged on her bottom lip with her teeth, and I groaned. Thank God the music was loud, and she hadn't heard me. I searched the crowded space for Cade and laughed. He had two gorgeous girls all over him.

Josie palmed my hard dick, then giggled. "I

was going to ask if you enjoyed dancing with me, but it's obvious you do."

I gawked at her. I'd never treat a girl like she was treating me, and I wasn't cool with getting fondled by a stranger. Stepping away from her, I gently took her by the shoulders. "Josie, you're attractive and I'm sure you're a great person, but I'm not interested in a one-night stand … or anything for that matter."

Her hands fell to her sides, and she glared at me. "What kind of loser doesn't fuck a girl when she throws herself at him?"

Wow. She was definitely more than I'd bargained for. "A guy that actually cares about your well-being. I don't sleep with anyone when they're wasted."

She snorted and stomped her foot. Images of Cassie at the frat party flickered through my mind. No, thank you. Girls who behaved like they were a toddler weren't my thing.

Josie folded her arms across her ample chest and stuck her lower lip out. I wasn't sure if she thought I'd find that attractive or what, but I backed away immediately. It was time for another drink, then I'd check to see if there was a pool table open.

After I'd found a spot to hide, I'd regretted coming out. I had no idea where Cade was, but I could take a wild guess that he and the girls had headed out. He knew he couldn't bring them to my place, but Cade didn't care where he got laid as long as it happened. For now, I was on my own.

I approached a pool table and watched the four guys that were in the middle of a game. One of them nodded at me. "You want to play the winner?" he asked.

"Yeah, that'd be great. Thanks." I propped one foot against the wall and waited for my turn, tapping my foot to the song the band was playing.

Over the next hour, I hung out with the group and played pool. The alcohol had hit me, and I was feeling more relaxed. As I leaned over the pool table to aim, an odd movement caught my eye. I jerked my head up and blinked, attempting see better. Quickly making the shot, I moved back and scanned the room. Once again, I attempted to clear my vision in case it had just lied to me. This couldn't be fucking happening.

27

Nearly jumping over the table, I realized I still had the pool stick in my hand and quickly handed it to the dark-haired guy next to me. "Thanks, I've gotta go, guys." Without waiting for a response, I moved as fast as possible toward the front door. Surely, I'd been mistaken, and the alcohol was messing with me. After all, the place was packed, the lights were low, and everyone looked the same after a few drinks. Since I rarely drank, Cade and John gave me shit about being a lightweight, and I regretted my drink choices at the moment.

I stepped outside into the chilly evening air. The overhead streetlamps illuminated the parking lot, and my gaze darted around the shadows, but I didn't see anyone. The hair on my neck stood on end and chills skated down my spine. My senses were on high alert, and I needed to always trust my instincts.

As I rounded the corner of the building, my attention landed on Brandon Montgomery. He was practically dragging Josie with him, her arms hanging loosely at her sides and her head rolling from side to side. I wasn't sure if she was drunk or drugged, but it didn't matter. I knew exactly what the son of a bitch had planned. Sweat beaded on the nape of my neck, and my pulse throbbed wildly as I crept closer. As far as I could tell, Brandon wasn't aware that I had followed them. The element of surprise was in my favor, and I needed to make sure I didn't lose my edge. Unfortunately I had to wait until I saw he was about to assault her. Otherwise, he could press charges against me for attacking him.

Brandon stopped, then propped Josie's limp body against the club's red-and-white brick wall. A small moan escaped her parted lips. Brandon held her up with one hand and tugged on the waistband of her jeans with the other. He managed to pull them down to her knees.

This fucking bastard made me sick. Bile crept

up my throat, and the acid burned my esophagus, and I choked it down.

My adrenaline kicked into high gear as I sprinted toward Brandon, knocking him off balance when I rammed my shoulder into his side.

"Motherfucker!" Brandon yelled, flailing around like a windsock on a windy day before he landed on his ass with a thud.

"Shut up, you little fucker." The promise I'd made to Dad was now null and void. I'd just caught Brandon trying to rape an unconscious girl. Josie's body slid down the side of the brick building and to the ground, but she didn't move. Removing my phone from my pocket, I began to dial 911, but Brandon scrambled to his feet and charged me. My cell flew through the air and landed with a clatter on the pavement.

"Stay out of my business, Harrington." Spittle shot from Brandon's mouth as he pinned me against the unforgiving ground and struck my cheek with his fist. Rage bubbled up inside me. I'd tried to be nice, but he wasn't leaving me any choice. His time was officially up.

I bucked my hips, knocking him off me, then flipped him over onto his back. Without talking myself out of it, I punched him in the mouth. "That's for Eva." My fist connected with his nose, and blood spurted in every direction. "That's for Mac." I pummeled him a few more times, anger driving each strike. "That's for Josie and every other girl you've drugged and raped, you stupid fucking shit."

"Hendrix!"

My name barely registered in my head as I landed another hit into Brandon's bloody and busted face.

"Dude, you're going to get arrested. You've gotta stop before you kill him." Fingers dug into my shoulders and jerked me off Brandon.

Not realizing who had put their hands on me, I spun around and threw a punch, stopping inches away from Cade's nose. *Fuck!*

"Hey!" Cade knocked my hand away, then gently slapped my cheek a few times, attempting to snap me out of my adrenaline induced fury.

From the corner of my eye, I spotted Brandon on the ground, groaning in pain. I spit near Brandon's shoes, letting him know exactly what I thought of him. Everything inside me wanted to end his pathetic rapist life, but it wasn't who I was. I only fought if I had no other choice. Catching him in the act was all the justification I'd needed.

I nodded at Cade, coming out of my anger-driven haze a little. "Josie needs help. Call 911." Glancing over my shoulder, I caught a glimpse of the girl that had nearly been sexually assaulted. She was still crumpled on the ground, unconscious. A crowd of people gathered around as Cade knelt next to Josie and called for help.

I approached Brandon, who was standing slowly. My breaths came in jagged and erratic spurts as I mentally considered a hit to his kidneys. Cade was right though, I had to stop. I'd accomplished what I'd needed to, which was stopping Brandon from raping another innocent victim.

Brandon staggered toward me, blood dripping from his nose and the cut on his forehead. His left eye was nearly swollen shut, and his grey shirt was smeared with dirt and torn. Brandon's light brown hair stuck up in the back. If I hadn't still been so pissed, I would have lost my shit and laughed my ass off. Brandon looked absolutely hideous. I'd worked him over good.

Brandon drug his feet along the asphalt, each step closing the distance between us. I stood my ground as he closed the gap between us, willing him to throw a punch in my direction.

He sneered at me, hatred darkening his expression. "You've fucked up now, Harrington." He jabbed a long finger into my chest.

Brandon had five seconds to back the fuck off, or he wouldn't be able to walk when I was finished with him. The paramedics would have to scoop him off the ground to place him on a gurney.

Brandon released a coldhearted chuckle, and it filled the small space between us. His gaze narrowed, and the snarl on his lips shot chills down my spine.

"I'm going to destroy you and everyone you love. Just when you think I've forgotten all about tonight … that's when I'll rip everything away from you one by one until I bring you to your knees begging and pleading for me to show mercy. And rest assured I won't. Not until I've destroyed you. Mark my words, Harrington." The layers of inhibition he'd cloaked himself in shed like a snake's skin, leaving him exposed and revealing his true form.

His words sent a jolt of anger through me. Before I could stop myself, my fist flew into his nose. The motherfucker's neck snapped back, and he dropped to the ground like a limp noodle. "I'll be waiting for you." I kicked his leg, but he didn't move.

WHEN DAD SHOWED up at Jimmy Z's, I couldn't tell if he was pissed or not. Cade had called him once the cops had shown up and arrested me. The second I was cuffed and tossed in the back of the squad car, reality bitch-slapped me in the face. As much as Cade tried to explain to the police what had happened, they weren't ready to hear my side of the story yet. I watched through the slightly tinted window as two ambulances arrived and loaded Josie and Brandon into separate ones, then left for the hospital. Since I'd stopped Josie from being raped, there wasn't any physical evidence, only my word against Brandon's. Hatred for that asshole stirred deep inside me.

I shifted on the hard leather seat of the cruiser, and attempted to see around the crowd of people, but there were too many now. A bright white flash broke through the darkness and temporarily blinded me. Ducking my head, I swore underneath my breath. The fucking press was here.

Seconds later, the media was told to clear out and the back door of the cop car opened. I sucked in the cool, fresh air and dared to glance up.

"Let's go." The short male officer motioned for

me to get out. I stood, staring at Charles and Dad for a moment. "You're lucky your dad is an attorney," the cop mumbled.

I met his comment with silence. Dad had taught me that if I ever got into trouble to shut the fuck up. The officer stepped behind me, the click of the handcuffs popping open was music to my ears. I immediately rubbed my wrists.

"Son," Dad said. He lifted his brow at me, and I understood all the words he hadn't spoken but conveyed perfectly. Not only was he pissed, but he was also disappointed in me.

Dad squeezed my arm and guided me away from the police. Cade joined us on my right side, and I grimaced at him. He discreetly nodded at me. Quickly peering over my shoulder, I admitted defeat. Charles was directly on my heels, ensuring the press wasn't following me. But it was too late, and I knew it. Pictures of my arrest were most likely already splashed all over the internet.

"Is the bar pressing charges since we were on their property?" I asked Dad, dreading his response. But deep down inside me, I didn't regret beating the hell out of Brandon. Once we had some privacy, I planned on explaining to Dad exactly what had happened so we could clear up this shitshow.

Dad continued to lead us to the car without a word. Maybe he was afraid of being overheard.

Feeling like a little kid on the way to the principal's office, I scuffed my tennis shoes against the pavement. Dad sure as hell hadn't ever taken any interest when I'd gotten in trouble at school. It wasn't often, but he was always too drunk to show up and be a parent anyway. So why now? I was twenty years old and had just saved a girl from being raped.

I stared into the darkness ahead, then stopped abruptly, snapping to attention. *No fucking way.* "Dad, you're shittin' me, right?"

28

$\mathcal{D}$ad released me as we reached the car. "Rest assured, Hendrix, I'm in no way shitting you." Dad's words were clipped. He was super pissed.

Another bodyguard stood near a second Mercedes, patiently waiting for us to reach the vehicle. Like Charles, he was over six feet tall, a solid wall of muscle with broad shoulders. The breeze ruffled his short blonde hair, and his honey-colored eyes were alert and trained on me as I approached him.

Where did Dad find these guys? Both Charles and his co-worker looked like they had walked off the cover of GQ.

"Hendrix, meet Jackson Sullivan, your new bodyguard."

My nostrils flared. How dare Dad make this decision without hearing me out about what had happened tonight. "Cade, Charles will bring you to our place. I need to have a private discussion with my son on the way home."

Cade grimaced. "Yes, sir." He mouthed sorry as he climbed into the back of the black Mercedes and Charles hopped into the driver's side.

Pissed didn't even begin to describe how I felt right now. I jumped into the back seat, counting to ten in my head. Once we were on the road and, I faced Dad. "That's it? You think since you bought me a house you own me? You haven't even asked me what happened. You just showed up with a bodyguard and assumed I was in the wrong." I clamped my mouth closed before I said something I couldn't take back. "I thought we were building some trust between us. It's obvious it's one sided and I was mistaken." The muscles in my neck knotted as I gripped the car door, swallowing back the scream that was building in my chest.

"We'll discuss it when we're home, Hendrix."

I shook my head and stared out the window. With each pine and cedar tree that passed by, I reminded myself that I was capable of supporting myself and standing on my own two feet. I hadn't needed Dad since I was a kid. He'd never taken care of me. It had always been the other way around. Fear wrapped its hand around my throat, threatening to choke the life-sustaining air from me. The worst part of the rude awakening I'd received that night was that I wanted him to be the dad he was pretending to be. But wanting and needing were two different things. My chest ached with Dad's hollow words he'd slung around the last few months. He hadn't changed. He might be sober, but he was still a fucking asshole.

As soon as I had my new keys, I was out of there. I'd pay him back every goddamned penny he'd paid for it, too. I sure as hell wouldn't make the same mistake twice either. In that moment, I promised myself I'd never accept Dad's help again. We were over. It was clear where his allegiance really was, and it wasn't with me. He would always be a self-serving prick.

What felt like an eternity later, Jackson parked the car in front of the garage. I jumped out, then let myself into the house. Dad closed the front door, the click echoing through the marble foyer.

"My office."

I shoved my hands in my pocket. For the first

time since I'd beat the shit out of Brandon, my arms and legs screamed at me. There was no telling what my face looked like, either. Brandon had hammered a few good hits to me as well. My chest warmed with the image of that sick bastard lying on the ground unconscious. I didn't give a fuck what came out of Dad's mouth. I didn't regret my choice tonight. Even the media could be spun correctly if he chose to interfere.

The picture of Dad and me laughing together at the beach when I was four rested on Dad's bookshelf. My stomach soured. The only real thing about him was his amazing ability to fake that he cared about me or anyone else.

I sank into the black leather wingback chair and remained quiet. I'd already decided we were done. This conversation was only an empty formality.

Dad closed the door behind him, walked to his cherrywood executive desk, removed a key from his pocket, and unlocked a drawer. He pulled out a file and placed it on top of his laptop.

"I couldn't discuss anything in front of Jackson or Charles. Cade can't know about this either, Hendrix. Besides, if this conversation gets heated, I wanted to feel as though we had some privacy." He sank wearily into his seat, his words bouncing right off me as anger took root again.

My mouth opened and Dad held his hand up, halting me. "Before I say anything else, yes, I'm angry. You put yourself into the middle of a dangerous situation ... but I'm proud of you."

Huh? I glanced over my shoulder, double-checking that he was actually talking to me. "I'm confused."

"I would have done the exact same thing, Hendrix. You stopped a rape in progress." Dad paused, his attention falling to the folder. "But." Dad laced his fingers together and leaned forward in his chair, lowering his voice. "Brandon is under investigation. What you saw tonight was an undercover agent, attempting to catch a serial rapist."

"Wait. What?"

Dad continued, ignoring my interruption. "I'm protecting you, son. I know it looked like I was mad, but I'm concerned that you might have gotten yourself tangled up in this case. The last thing I want is for the FBI to use you as an asset."

Holy fucking shit.

I blinked excessively, staring at him in shock.

Feeling like a complete and total asshole for the crap I'd thought about Dad earlier, I stared at him speechless. Guilt gnawed at me as I tried to form a sentence, but I was grasping for straws. Brandon was lowlife scum, but never in a million years would I have suspected the FBI was interested in him.

"The FBI took care of the media. Your almost arrest won't be broadcast in any way. They're also trying to keep Josie's identity under wraps." Dad leaned back in his chair, rocking gently. "I don't know what Josie's real name is, and I don't want to. I am aware that this is much bigger than Brandon."

I swallowed hard. "Bigger?" I asked, finally able to articulate a word.

"Obviously the FBI won't tell me anything else. They made it clear that you have to stay out of the situation, or they will use you."

"Dammit." I scrubbed my face, wishing the nightmare away. "All I wanted to do was stop him from hurting another girl, Dad." The corners of my mouth twitched slightly, but I suppressed my grin. "And beat the shit out of him for what he did to Eva and Mac."

"I know, and honestly, I was cheering you on. The bastard deserved everything he got tonight."

I leaned forward, propping my elbows on my

knees. "Why did you act like you were pissed at me all the way home?"

"I'm angry at the situation and scared that you might have landed in the middle of it. As I said, I couldn't talk to you in front of Charles, Jackson, or Cade. This can't be discussed outside of this room. Am I clear?"

"Yeah." I rolled all of this new information around in my head. "Josie is an agent?" I chuckled. "Dad she was all over me tonight. She was ready to ..." I cleared my throat. "I told her no because she was drunk. A girl that wasted is off limits for me no matter how much I want to get laid."

"You're a smart man. What you didn't realize is that Josie had seen Brandon. She's well aware of the mutual hate you two have for each other. You were bait."

"I can't believe this." I leaned back and ran my hands through my hair. "I'm done with the female population. I'm recommitting myself to my career."

Dad attempted to hide his smile. "When the right girl shows up and holds your heart in her hand, I'm going to remind you of this conversation."

"Good luck with that. From now on, I'm

staying as far away from Brandon as possible and working on my music. Between that and school, hopefully I'll manage to stay out of trouble."

A heavy silence hung over us. "I'm really sorry about tonight, Hendrix. My job is to protect you and I've let you down for so long. I realize you're grown and can take care of yourself, but I didn't want the media twisting that story, either. Your career is taking off, and I'm finally in the position of helping. Please know that your safety and happiness will always be my main priority."

My heart jumped into my throat and my shoulders slumped forward, my feelings spinning around and twisting my insides into knots. "I'm sorry I got angry and thought shitty things about you tonight." To my surprise Dad threw his head back and laughed. I wasn't sure what was so funny, though. I'd just admitted how pissed I'd been at him.

"I'm sure you did. Hendrix, I know it's going to take time for you to trust me. No matter what a situation might appear to be, I'll always have your back. You're my son and the reason I'm alive." Tears welled in his eyes. "You're the reason I got sober, Hendrix."

29

$\mathcal{I}$ stared at him, afraid to speak. Surely he hadn't admitted that *I* was the reason he'd stopped drinking. I'd spent my entire life feeling as though I wasn't enough for him to get his life together.

"Me?" I whispered, blinking back the tears.

"Yes. I know that for most of your life I was a pathetic drunk, but when I realized what an amazing young man you've turned into ..." Dad sniffed. "I couldn't continue to not be a part of your life."

Overcome with disbelief and something that felt an awful lot like hope, silent tears streamed down my cheeks. After all the years of me taking care of him, cleaning him up, begging him to stop drinking … somehow, he'd finally heard me. Somewhere inside him I'd helped him start recovery.

"As honest as you've been with me tonight, I'm going to be honest with you too. If you ever drink again, I'm done. We're done. My heart is fragile, dangling by a thread. Every day I hope that you're becoming the father I've always wanted, and now … Now I have a taste of who that man is. I'm terrified that you have the ability to destroy me, and I don't know what to do with that. I know we're making progress, but we have a ways to go." I steepled my hands together. "Please, don't let either of us down. I will support you in any way I can, but we both know it's ultimately your choice." I dropped my hands, stood, and approached him. "Love you, Dad," I whispered.

Dad stood and wrapped me up in a huge hug. "I love you too, Hendrix."

"Hey," I said, joining Cade in the game room upstairs after I had a few minutes to myself to digest the information Dad had shared with me.

He was stretched out along the leather couch, his feet dangling off the end. "Dude, what went down between you and your dad?" Cade dropped a bag of Doritos to the floor and sat up, removing the white AirPods from his ears.

I yawned as I sank onto the floor. "It's all been taken care of. The band won't get any bad press."

Cade narrowed his eyes at me, disbelief clouding his expression. "You mean Brandon trying to rape that girl has been swept under the rug?" Cade's tone carried a hint of frustration.

"Pretty much. Dad took care of the press. He didn't want August Clover to get caught in a media frenzy." I couldn't tell Cade the FBI had actually stepped in and taken care of the situation.

Cade searched my face. "And? I mean I understand and I'm grateful for his help about the arrest, but you caught Brandon in the act of raping someone."

I mentally chewed on my next words. There was no way I wanted to be involved with the FBI and the case. Hell, I wasn't even sure what it was all about. The last thing I could do was talk to Cade about it. "It's out of my hands. The police have the information and Dad will do what he can, but it's not up to us at this point." I inwardly sighed with relief that I hadn't lied to my best friend.

"Wait until John hears about all the shit that

went down tonight." Cade shook his head. "How did you even know Brandon was there?"

I laced my fingers behind my head. "As crowded as that place was tonight, I caught a glimpse of Brandon. It was so quick, I thought I'd imagined it, but it looked like he was leaving with a girl. I couldn't let that shit go, so I hauled ass out the front door and searched for him." A low chuckle rumbled in my chest. "I obviously found him." My smile fell away as I recalled Brandon's threat. Excitement and fear battled for control within me. If he followed through, I'd make sure he regretted every minute of fucking with me.

"He swore that he'd destroy me and everyone I love." A rock formed in the pit of my stomach. "He might be crazy enough to do it, too."

Cade's intense amber-colored eyes connected with mine. "You just made Brandon your enemy for life, dude. Let's hope he gets distracted along the way." Cade tapped the side of his head. "I think something is broken up here. He's not the guy we hung out with in our freshman and sophomore year in high school."

As much as I wanted to disagree with Cade, I couldn't. "Even from the time we were boxing together he's changed. I have no idea what happened, but I think it's worse than I thought."

Anxiety pulled and tugged at my insides. At the same time, I'd had a twisted satisfaction when I'd beaten his ass earlier.

"We'll make an effort to steer clear and maybe Brandon will lose his hard-on for you. Let's stay focused on what's important and let the police do their job."

My cell phone buzzed in my back pocket, and I leaned over on one hip and removed it.

Dude! I'm not with you for one night and you and Brandon fight? This is what I get for having to work. Ugg.

I glanced at Cade and grinned. "Mac's mad she missed the shitshow tonight."

"She was better off not being involved." Cade leaned his head back on the couch and averted his gaze, but not before I saw the fierce protectiveness flash across his face.

I typed Mac a quick response that I'd fill her in tomorrow. I hadn't realized it was almost three in the morning. My ass was exhausted.

"I'll grab some blankets and pillows." I stood and a prickle of dread danced across my skin. If anything happened to Cade or John because I stood up to Brandon, I wasn't sure how I'd live with myself. It was one thing if he came after me. Another if he came after the people I loved. With the FBI involved, I suspected Brandon and whatever else he was mixed up in was more dangerous than I could begin to wrap my head around.

It might be up to Dad to protect me, but it was my job to protect the people I loved, especially if my actions set hell into motion. I wasn't interested in dancing with the devil when I'd just landed on my feet after the last several years with Dad. It was my turn now to have the life I wanted, free of guilt and heartache.

"Do you need anything else?" I peered over at my best friend and laughed softly as Cade responded with a soft snore.

30

The summer passed without any more incidents from Brandon, but I steered clear of him. Rumors ran rampant of his sexual activities, including rough sex, BDSM, and threesomes. Some girls participated willingly, and some didn't.

John returned home after six weeks in Montana. Eva and John had agreed the time wasn't right for a relationship. Eva struggled with reliving Brandon's sneer and the drugged sensation. She thought she could move through it, but she needed more time to heal. I suspected John did too.

At least John had taken the time to spend with her. Even if he realized Eva wasn't the girl for him, he wouldn't wonder what could have happened between them. It had still messed him up, though, and he was making up for lost time. He and Cade were constantly hooking up with nameless women after our performances. As long as they were discreet and didn't cause bad press, I didn't give a rat's ass.

Mac stayed busy at work and took extra shifts to pay me back for fixing her car. Honestly, I didn't care if she paid me back or not, but it was important to her, so I accepted the money.

I finally sat down and told Mac about Eva's struggle. Although it hurt Mac that Eva blamed her for Brandon's behavior, deep down Mac knew she'd done everything she could. She wasn't surprised that Eva was having a difficult time moving on after the assault either. John sat down with Mac and they had a long talk about what had happened with Eva, too. It seemed to help both of them process the loss of their friend and someone they both loved.

I slid the glass door open and stepped out onto the back patio of my house. School would start next week, and I'd invited everyone over for dinner. Cade and John were at my place nearly every day, but when they left, the silence was nearly deafening. For the first time in my life, I wasn't surrounded by other people and messes I had to fix. I was left alone with only my thoughts. Sometimes it scared me.

The sound of the doorbell caught my attention, and I hurried to the front door and flung it open. I grinned at the man in front of me. "Hey, Dad. Glad you could come over a little early."

Dad chuckled as he handed me a large bowl of fresh salad. "Me too, son. Ruby made that for your BBQ." Dad held up a reusable bag with handles. "This is her version of Death by Chocolate that you all love."

I groaned and licked my lips. "Man, I think I could eat that for dinner all by itself."

Dad closed the door behind him and chuckled. "I'm pretty sure you'd be hurling before the night was over. It's super rich."

I walked to the kitchen and set the large bowl on the tan marble countertop.

"The kitchen looks amazing. I love that you chose the cherry cabinets, too. I bet you're happy to have all of the upgrades finished." Dad set the bag on the counter and smiled.

"I'm glad I don't live in a construction zone anymore. I wouldn't have been able to study," I laughed and nodded at the refrigerator.

"Drinks are in the fridge. I grabbed some of your favorite."

Dad shot me a confused look, then checked for himself. His laughter filled my house and my heart. "Orange Crush, huh? It's been years. Thanks." He popped the tab and the hiss of the carbonation filled the room, then he smiled.

"Everyone will be here in half an hour. Do you want to sit outside for a bit?" I hesitated. "Is Charles out there?"

"He is." Dad took a drink, then a boyish smile eased across his face.

"Alright, I'll make him and Jackson a steak too, then." The bodyguards pulled long hours and were constantly working. The least I could do was cook them a nice meal on occasion.

I'd still not gotten used to Jackson lurking around, but he remained outside most of the time. At least this way I still had some privacy, but I wasn't sure what having a bodyguard would look like when I started classes. I was hoping to ditch him, but I needed to talk to Dad first.

A warm September breeze blew off the river, rustling the tree leaves in the yard. Once Dad and I were settled outside and seated, I spotted Jackson near the side of the house. "Have you heard any updates?" I asked in a hushed voice. "About Brandon, I mean?"

"No, just that the investigation is ongoing." Dad crossed his legs and rested his soda on his jeaned thigh.

"Is there a possibility that things have settled down some and I don't have to have Jackson at school with me?"

Dad pursed his lips. "I'm concerned, son. Brandon will return this school year, and he threatened you."

I shifted in my chair. "The likelihood that he would cross a line with me in public with witnesses is slim. It would blow up in his face. Personally, I'd be fine with that. The sooner he's gone from our life, the better."

"Since he hasn't sought you out, I'm thinking you're fine at school, but Hendrix …" Dad leaned forward, his blue eyes narrowing with concern. "You have to tell me if there's even a hint of trouble. I'm really serious."

A flicker of fear danced across Dad's features. He took another drink, then continued. "At that point, Jackson or someone will join you again. I have to make sure you're safe. If I have your word, then we can try it."

"I promise." Although I wasn't crazy about the

idea of a bodyguard again, I wasn't stupid. Brandon was sneaky, and I didn't want to let my guard down.

Dad released a sigh. "I'll admit that this decision is going against my better judgement, but we'll see how it plays out. You're very capable of protecting yourself. I just don't want you to get sucked into whatever is going on. All I can say is that it's really big, son."

"What's that?" Mac asked, stepping out onto the patio.

"Hey! I didn't hear you." I stood and wrapped her in a big hug.

"I rang the doorbell a few times, but I'm guessing your sliding glass door has some noise deadening shit in it." Mac glanced at Dad and grimaced. "Sorry. I'll watch my mouth."

I chuckled. Mac was always apologizing for swearing, but never seemed to be able to stop herself.

Seconds later, John and Cade caught my attention through the glass of the slider and strolled into the house. "The guys are here. I'll get the steaks started."

Over the next several hours, we all laughed and reminisced about high school and college days. John, Cade, and I worked out a time to help

Mac move into her dorm on Monday as well. She was excited and nervous about her freshman year. I felt like it would be good for me to know she was on campus with us. I'd missed her while she was still in high school. The guys obviously did too because they were constantly picking on her that night.

The best part of the evening was having Dad with us. Although he didn't share as many of the memories with us, he was creating new ones that I'd cherish for the rest of my life. He was quickly earning everyone's respect, including mine. It was crazy how close we'd grown over the last year and a half.

He'd even confided in me about returning to his practice. As long as he stayed sober, I'd support anything he wanted to do. Besides, even when he was a drunk, he was a damn good attorney. My only fear was how skilled he was at hiding his drinking, and I no longer lived with him. On those days when the memories and darkness seized me, I had to remind myself that Dad was no longer my responsibility, and I had a good life ahead of me. It eased the anxiety a little, but it would take a long time for me to settle into our new relationship.

I kicked back as the stars began to light up the

night sky. The sound of the river brought me back to reality, and once again I was grateful for my own sanctuary. It was the cocoon I could retreat to at any time. Now that the construction was over, I'd be able to relax more, which meant writing music. That night, my heart was full of love and appreciation for the family that was spending time with me. I was amazed and grateful with how much my life had changed.

31

ONE YEAR LATER

"*D*ude, I hope my roomie is better than the one in my freshman year." Mac rolled her eyes and slapped her palm against her forehead. "Ohmigosh, she was a sex addict, or a nymph, or whatever the hell they call people like her. Like how many guys can you fuck in one night? Eww."

I suppressed my chuckle as Mac and I walked across the college campus together. "You can stay at my house any time you need to." I glanced down at her and smiled. At times I wondered if this girl knew how much I adored her.

Mac scrunched up her nose. "I can't even stand to think about how many times they used my bed. When I'd go back to the room, I'd rip all the bedding off and Lysol my mattress."

"That's bullshit. No one should have to deal with that. There's a thing called respect and hygiene."

Mac nodded enthusiastically. "I can't believe I'm already a sophomore and you're a junior. I feel old." Mac heaved a dramatic sigh, hooking her thumbs on the bib of her overalls. Somehow Mac always looked adorable in them, but I don't think most girls could pull off the look.

I draped my arm around her shoulders as I drank in the late September sunshine while the grass softly crunched beneath my tennis shoes. This time of year, the trees and ground were brown and dry, pleading for water in order to survive. However, the campus was well maintained, which was nice.

A heavy silence descended over us. Neither of us wanted to mention the bastard that consumed too much head space in our minds. Brandon Montgomery. Last year he'd gone on a rampage and way too many girls stepped up and attempted to press charges against him for rape, but each time it was swept under the rug.

"How's the new song coming along?" Mac leaned her head against me. "Your songs are fucking amazing, so stop doubting yourself and write more. When the girls don't cream their panties over the lyrics, your voice will give them orgasms. I mean, like, why would you ever second-guess yourself?"

I rolled my eyes at her. Mac's lack of a filter cracked me up most of the time. "I don't think I have that effect on the ladies, but thanks for the vote of confidence." I smoothed my basic white T-shirt. For some reason I wanted to keep it super casual today.

"You slay me. You're so fucking hot, a boxer badass, you're a gentleman, and you can sing. Ohmigosh can you sing." Mac shivered slightly. "Your tone is rich and dripping with sexiness." Mac giggled as she pretended to swoon and dramatically fanned herself.

A laugh bellowed from my chest. "I love you." I placed a kiss on the top of her head. "Thanks for being my biggest fan. I couldn't do it without you."

Mac abruptly stopped. "You're my Superman, Hendrix. You've been there for me when no one else showed up. You helped me when I lost my best friend and after Brandon attacked my car with a bat. I'm your biggest fan because I see how amazing you are on so many levels." Mac threw her arms around me.

"I'm your biggest fan, too," I whispered against her soft hair.

"Ahh, shucks." She moved back, then whacked me on my chest with the back of her hand.

A phone buzzed and we both checked our cells. "It's me." She waved hers in front of me.

I waited while Mac took her call. A huge grin spread across her face, then she hung up. "Ohmigosh. That was Savannah Compton, my friend from art class. My new roomie is lost, and Savannah asked if I could pick her up from the student center." Mac pushed up on her tiptoes and kissed my cheek. "Later!" She took off sprinting across the campus lawn toward the parking lot.

It was good to see Mac happy again. Between losing Asher and Eva, the last year had been hard on her. Mac had confided in me that Asher messaged her on occasion. After three years together, it seemed he was struggling with the breakup as well. Unfortunately, Asher's father had gotten involved and ended the relationship. The entire situation had been fucked up.

After John had returned from his summer with

Eva, Mac had started picking up the pieces of her heart and looking forward instead of back. Once in a while she'd confide in me how much it still stung, but she refused to try to convince Eva to remain her friend. Eva never gave her the opportunity to share her side of the story and what had happened after she'd found Brandon assaulting her. In my opinion, Eva hadn't really valued Mac's friendship. Maybe she'd been shallow all along and we were just now seeing it. I wouldn't dismiss the possibility that what Brandon had done to Eva had changed her into something different. I wasn't sure.

A soft breeze lifted the strands of my shoulder-length brown hair, and I lifted my face to the sun. Since the rest of my afternoon was open, I decided to see if my favorite writing spot was available. Last year no one had bothered me there, but it seemed as though there were a lot more people on campus that day.

I took my time and walked to the library. When no one was paying attention, I ducked behind the building. To my relief, no one was back there. No matter where I went, I carried a notebook and pen with me. Inspiration had hit me in some strange places, and I had finally learned to be prepared. However, I'd struggled with writer's block for the last several weeks. I blamed it on the start of the school year, but I highly doubted it had anything to do with it. The real culprit had been Brandon. His threats from last year still lingered in my mind, jabbing at my vulnerabilities when I least expected it. The closer it got to the new school year, the more his words taunted me.

I'd steered clear of him most of the time, but on occasion we'd see each other. He'd sneer at me and point to his eyes with his first two fingers, then at me. Brandon had made it clear he hadn't forgotten his promise and he was watching. If the FBI wasn't involved, I would have already taken matters into my own hands, but this was much bigger than my own desires. I still didn't have a clue why the FBI was interested in Brandon, but I didn't want to know.

I sank onto the grass. The constant sounds of chatter drifted away as I began to relax and block out the people on campus.

Removing my pen from the spiral spine of my notebook, I began to tap out a rhythm on my jeaned thigh. Once the beats took on a life of their own, I flipped to a blank page ... and stared at it. I leaned my head against the side of the brick building, willing the words to show up. Nothing. I groaned in frustration. How in the hell was I supposed to write August Clover's next song if my creativity had flipped me off and left me high and dry?

Lost in thought and throwing insults at myself for lack of focus, I was surprised when a figure darted around the corner of the library and fell to the ground. Startled, I remained still, witnessing the moments unfold in front of me, completely unaware of how they would affect me for the rest of my life.

At first I wasn't sure if it was a guy or girl. They'd moved so quickly around the building I hadn't been able to see them clearly. A floppy denim hat covered their head, hiding their identity from me.

Long, thin fingers dug into the ground and a soft cry escaped the person in front of me. I stood quietly, not wanting to scare them. Before I could make my presence known, the figure stood. A wisp of hair had escaped the hat, but the sun captured the strands in the brilliant afternoon light, but I couldn't tell what color it was.

I reached out, then changed my mind. The small frame trembled beneath oversized and worn clothes. By the looks of the hands, it was a girl. A terrified one. My heart hammered in my chest. Was she hurt?

I watched her fingers ball into fists as she

squared her shoulders and sucked in a deep breath. She tilted her chin up, then disappeared around the corner of the building. I'd just witnessed her having a full-on panic attack, then pull herself together in a matter of seconds. Maybe some people would have seen her actions as weak, but I didn't. She had the courage to pick herself off the ground and face the world again. I knew firsthand how hard that was.

My heart pitter-pattered against my chest. *Ugh. What the hell was I doing?* I'd been so mesmerized by her strength I'd lost my mind. *Go after her!*

I flew around the corner of the building and searched the area, but I didn't see the denim hat in the crowd anywhere. Chiding myself for not thinking faster, I hurried up the steps of the library. Maybe she'd gone inside.

Pulling the front door open, the air conditioning greeted me as my shoes smacked against the tile floor, echoing through the entrance. My hand landed on the push bar and I barged into the quiet room. The librarian glared at me as I grimaced. In all of my excitement to find this girl, I hadn't realized how loud I was.

I remained near the entrance and scanned the tables. Seconds later, I spotted her, and my pulse stuttered against my wrist. Even inside she kept the hat on, but this time I realized she also wore dark tinted glasses. Dammit, I'd hoped to be able to see her eyes.

Before I spoke to her, I took a minute to collect my thoughts. What was this girl's story? Was she recovering from cancer, or did she have a rare disease? Maybe she couldn't be exposed to the sunlight. I instinctively knew the answer already. She was hiding from someone, but who?

32

*C*aptivated, I walked closer to her. Her foot tapped beneath the table, and I realized she had headphones in her ears. Trying not to startle her, I placed my hand on the cool wooden surface in front of her. When she still didn't look up, I tapped a finger next to her book.

She jerked her hand away from mine and her head snapped up.

From what I could see of her face, which wasn't much, she was highly irritated that I'd interrupted her. Most of the time it would have deterred me, but I was more intrigued than before.

A slight smattering of freckles covered her perky little nose and cheekbones, highlighting her porcelain skin. Her clothes swallowed her, but I could still tell she was petite. From the quick glimpse I'd had of her standing, she was taller than Mac. Her full lips were the perfect color of red and I suddenly found myself wondering what she would taste like if I kissed her. She folded her hands as I sat down at the other side of the table.

I flipped my hair over my shoulder, then motioned for her to remove the earbuds.

"What?" she asked, her tone bordering on the rude side.

"Are you okay?" I asked gently. Whatever she'd been through, she was scared and hid behind a tough exterior. She just didn't know that I'd done the same for years, and I could see right through it.

Her eyebrows knitted together in confusion. "Sure," she replied.

From the tightness of her shoulders, she obviously wanted me to leave, but I couldn't. All I wanted to know was if she was all right. I mentally kicked myself. I wanted more than that. I wanted to know who had hurt her. Brandon's name slithered across my mind, burning images of an unconscious Eva into it. Surely not, since this was the first day of school and from her thick Southern accent, she was new here.

"No, I'm serious. Are you okay? You almost

passed out behind the library. I was back there working on something," I said in a hushed tone.

Her mouth gaped slightly, then she slammed it closed. "I'm fine."

Heat spread across her neck and ears, giving away her true feelings. I'd just mortified this poor girl on accident.

We stared at each other silently, then she tilted her chin up in defiance. "There are plenty of other tables." She nodded toward them.

"Okay. I wanted to make sure you were all right. I didn't mean to bother you." I pushed the chair back and stood. "Nice glasses," I mumbled before walking away.

I peeked over my shoulder, hoping to catch a glimpse of her eyes, but she hadn't taken the glasses off. I'd hoped she would after my comment, but no such luck. I sat down at another table not far away from hers. Flipping open my notebook, I jotted down the first lyrics that had popped into my head in weeks. My head hung low, and I peered at her through the strands of my hair that partially hid my sight as I continued to write. I stole glances of the mystery girl while the words broke free inside me, begging to be sung.

Jesus. Whoever she was had helped me break

through my writer's block. Her quiet strength had pierced my soul. I recognized the pain and fear, yet she'd picked herself up off the ground and faced her ghosts. That wasn't weakness, that was determination. The same determination I'd had after I lost Kendra. Chaos slammed into me and caged me in my worst nightmare, the horror of that final day playing through my mind. *No!* Clenching my hands into fists, I willed myself to focus on reality. I refused to wallow in the past when my future was right in front of me. Whether she realized it or not, that girl was my hero.

Ten minutes later, she strolled by me on the way out of the library, and my gaze followed. Refusing to look like a stalker, I forced myself to continue sitting in my seat until I counted to a hundred. Slowly.

I had a suspicion that the library offered some type of comfort for her. It might take me a while, but I was bound and determined to find out who she was. An unfamiliar needle pricked my chest. As stupid as it sounded, I was afraid that girl had just walked away with my heart.

LATER THAT EVENING, Cade and John joined me at my house. "Is your dad coming over?" Cade asked, reaching into the kitchen cabinet in search of a glass.

"Nah. It's all good." I already understood what he was really asking.

John hopped off the barstool and headed to my garage where we had a hidden stash of beer and liquor. Dad hadn't ever shown up unannounced, but after the day he caught us drinking in his guesthouse, I'd gone to great lengths to keep any alcohol out of sight. He'd continued to stay sober, so it was my responsibility to support him.

"I'll take the good stuff tonight," I said, grinning at my friends.

Cade slid a tumbler down the countertop to me as John poured the amber-colored liquid into my glass.

"What's the occasion? You typically don't drink the hard stuff." John popped the top on a St. Pauli and leaned against the refrigerator, eyeing me suspiciously.

Cade joined me and poured some whiskey into his own glass.

"I met a girl." I couldn't stop the grin from spreading across my face.

Poor John nearly dropped his beer on the floor.

Cade glanced at John, then back to me. "Someone's got it bad," Cade said.

At first I thought he was teasing, but I wasn't sure how I could have it bad over a girl I'd barely spoken to and didn't really know what she looked like. My heart hammered against my chest, proving Cade right. "No, I don't have it *bad*. I'm ..." I tapped my chin with my finger. "I'm infatuated with her mysteriousness." I hadn't lied. It was true. But there was something special about her. Hell, I didn't even care about the big clothes, hat, and tinted glasses. I'd seen who she really was in those hidden moments behind the library.

"What's her name?" John asked.

I gave a half shrug and swirled the whiskey around in my glass, imagining what her name might be. "I don't know. I met her behind the library."

"Dude, you're hittin' it already?" Cade nearly choked on his drink.

An intense wave of protectiveness jolted through me and anger ignited my short fuse. "She had a panic attack and hid from someone behind the library, asshole."

The color drained from his cheeks. "I was just playin', man. I didn't mean anything by it."

Before I could say anything else, my phone buzzed against the counter. Mac's name popped up on the screen. I scooped it off the counter and read the message.

Dude! Love my roomie! We're going to be best friends!

It was only the first day of school, but I hoped Mac was right. She fell in love fast whether it was with a new friend or a guy, then she got her heart broken. It sucked watching her go through it, but I had mad respect for her because she loved with her whole heart. I wished the world had more people like Mac in it.

"It seems like Mac has a new best friend," I said to the guys.

"Yeah? She met her roommate?" John pushed off the fridge, then sat on a barstool beside mine.

"Yeah. I hope it works out better than it did last year," Cade added. "I didn't like how that girl treated Mac."

"None of us did," John added.

It had been a year since I'd noticed how much attention Cade paid to Mac, but he'd promised it was only friendship and nothing more. John had been the one to tell me to stay out of it. I had, but

I thought Cade would have found someone else by now. He certainly slept his way around Spokane, but so did John now. I was the only one out of the three of us that hadn't found anyone special enough to be with … until I saw her. But I hadn't just seen the mystery girl—her soul had touched mine.

I tapped out a quick response to Mac and told her I couldn't wait to meet her new roomie.

My cell buzzed again with her response.

She's super shy, so it might be a while.

I chuckled, almost feeling bad for the new girl. There was no such word as shy when it came to Mac.

"What else?" Cade asked, leaning on the counter.

I quirked an eyebrow at him as I took a drink. "What are you talking about? Mac?"

John snickered. "Nice try, Hendrix. Cade wants to know about the girl you met today."

I leaned back in my seat and folded my arms across my chest. "Honestly, there's not much to tell." After I explained how I met her, the guys stared at me with their mouths open.

"Let me get this straight," Cade started. "You're behind the library and this girl wearing baggy clothes, sunglasses, and a hat drops to the ground and has a panic attack in front of you? Then she walks off and you're head over heels for her?"

Dammit, I should have kept my mouth closed and not said anything to them yet.

"Sounds like you've got a savior complex," Cade added.

John shot out of his chair and grabbed my arm at the same time I jumped out of mine. I wrapped my fingers around my glass, willing my temper to calm down. These were my best friends and what I'd told them tonight sounded insane. Maybe it was, but I didn't give a fuck.

"No. You don't get it. Whatever happened to her ..." I sank back into my seat, my own memories stirring to life inside me. "She doesn't need saving. It's the opposite, Cade. She might have saved me."

John squeezed my shoulder as my words sank deep inside me. "After I saw her, I wrote a new song."

"The whole fucking thing?" John sat down again and took a drink of his beer.

"Yeah. I even have the melody in my head. I just need to get it on sheet music and play with it in a few spots. I've not been able to write like that in a long ass time."

Cade released a low whistle. "Damn. That's impressive. And to clear the air, I didn't mean anything by what I said earlier. If this girl is important to you, then she is to me as well. Besides, she's already done something right if you wrote a song today."

"No shit," John agreed. "I'm with Cade. If you're convinced she's someone special, then you've got my full support. No jokes about a savior complex or anything. You've got good judgement about people, so I'll be curious to see how it plays out."

"Same." Cade raised his tumbler. "To brotherhood and new beginnings."

We clinked our glasses and beer bottle together, then changed the conversation to the new song we were working on. As hard as I tried though, I couldn't dismiss the soft Southern drawl and the presence of the girl in the hat. There was no way I could know how much the girl in the glasses was about to change my life.

Enjoy a sneak peek of Love & Ruin.
Love & Ruin

I was no longer living. I was merely surviving.

Ada Lynn's worn rocking chair creaked as she rocked in a slow, steady rhythm on her front porch. She was nosy, but over the last four years, she'd become my only friend.

"Hello, Gemma." Her voice was strong, even though it shook slightly with age as it floated through the muggy, early evening air.

"Hey, Ada Lynn. How are you feeling today?" I pulled open the mailbox, the only extracurricular activity I had for the day. My eyes narrowed when I noticed a new splatter of bird crap that had graced the top of it. Reaching in, I removed the small bundle of letters.

"Well, not much has changed since yesterday. At my age, everything hurts."

The sky darkened briefly as a single white puffy cloud drifted across the late afternoon sun.

Weather permitting, she would lean on her cane, hobble outside, and sit every evening. She was one of the few people I'd spoken to in-person in five years—other than my parents. At nineteen, this would not be an easy feat for most. I found it easy after someone in the sleepy little town of

Breaux Bridge, Louisiana, stole my life, turning it into a shell of what it used to be.

"Whatcha got, there?" Ada Lynn's chin tilted up with her question.

I shuffled through the mail, my shoulders tensing when Hillview University's red, black, and white logo caught my eye. Raising my arm, I tucked the remainder of the stack into my armpit.

"Not sure." I ripped off one end of the envelope, flipped opened the note, and shook it free. The thin paper rustled in the soft breeze while I read it.

"Come on now, you can talk to ol' Ada Lynn. Something's got your goat, I can tell by the look on your face."

Folding the letter up quickly, I shoved it into the back pocket of my vastly oversized denim shorts. My T-shirt hung almost to my knees, so even if my shorts slipped some, no one would notice.

"Nothing, just junk." I brushed the stray red hairs out of my face that had escaped my ponytail and approached her chain link fence, smiling.

"You got a whole lot of junk there." She nodded toward my hand holding the additional mail.

"Everyone wants you to buy something, so

they pile up your box with nonsense. At least most of it's Mom and Dad's. All I get is an occasional credit card offer since I'm still at home."

Ada Lynn leaned back in her chair, her cloudy eyes critical as they traveled over me.

"When are you gonna wear some clothes that fit ya right and have some color? It's just the same drab, baggy stuff."

My gaze dropped to the cracked sidewalk beneath my sandaled feet for a moment and back to her.

"Never." My voice was strong and steady while I held her stare, challenging her to say more. Instead, her brown-eyed gaze softened.

"All right then. At least you're not prancing around like a little slut. Some of the girls these days... Well, we just never considered showing our bosoms in such a fashion." She pursed her lips in dissatisfaction and patted her recently styled gray curls.

I chewed on my thumbnail and grinned.

"Can I come up?"

"You know you don't have to ask. Come on, my blue-eyed girl," she replied, waving her hand and motioning for me to join her.

I unhooked the metal gate and strolled up the pitted and cracked walkway. I immediately made my way toward the seat next to her, as was our routine.

Ada Lynn at eighty-three was still mentally sharp. Nothing ever got by her, including me, and before I realized it, she had lifted my shirt and snatched the piece of paper out of my back pocket.

A heavy sigh escaped me as I plopped down in the chair next to her.

Ada Lynn scanned the paper, a solemn look on her face. She carefully stuffed it back in the envelope, handed it to me, and took my hand.

Silence hung in the air between us. I knew a lecture or pep talk was on the way.

"Saying it won't change anything, but it's not your business." I sighed and leaned my head back against the white rocker.

"Course it is. You're my business, Gemma Thompson."

Over the last few years, we'd grown close. Ada Lynn didn't have any children, and I didn't have any friends, so we were a perfect fit for each other.

"Someday I won't be here, so you've got to move on—keep going."

She wasn't saying anything I hadn't heard a

million times from her lips. Unfortunately, my parents weren't as encouraging.

"I'm trying," I muttered.

"Try harder." Her voice sounded clipped, stern with instruction. "Go to Washington and finish your degree."

"Maybe."

I grew quiet, my mind drifting between the past and the present. Sometimes I dared to dream a little, but then the memories crashed down on me like a tidal wave, crushing me again.

"This is your chance at a new life. Take it back, girl. *Take it back*," she whispered fiercely, squeezing my hand as though she could share her inner strength with me. If it'd been that easy, I would have already left this hellhole.

An hour passed while Ada Lynn and I sat together in complete silence other than the sounds of the insects coming alive for the evening. The clouds drifted across the sun; a whisper of another day was almost over.

A little later, a soft snore escaped Ada Lynn, and she jumped, waking herself.

"Shit," she said softly. "Fell asleep again, didn't I?"

"It's okay. I'm here." I gave her a gentle smile.

"I'd better go inside, and you'd better hurry

home before your parents start sniffing around looking for you. Help me in. I'll see you tomorrow." She offered a tired smile as I stood and held my hand out to her. If Ada Lynn sat too long, she struggled to get out of a chair on her own, so I always ensured she made it safely into her house.

I took her hand in mine, opened her front door, and helped her inside. Jesus extended his hand toward me, his heart glowing, as he welcomed me into her home from the obnoxious, bulky, plastic picture frame. Her living room never changed. The same bright orange and yellow colored afghan fell across the arm of the worn black leather couch. My pulse quickened while Ada Lynn turned toward me. I had a strong suspicion of what she was going to say, and I wasn't sure how I'd handle it.

"Be brave, Gemma." The thin, fragile skin of her hand felt like tissue paper as she touched my cheek. "Take the opportunity. I'll pay for your way out there and help you with some money until you're all settled. Do this for me, for an old woman with one last wish."

"I'll think about it." Tears blurred my vision, and I took a deep, shaky breath. I stepped back and attempted the best smile I had left inside me.

After locking the door behind me, my feet

hurried down the porch steps and next door to my house. The yellow paint had dulled over time and was now peeling. My parents hadn't found the time to change it to a more appealing color. This was the only house I had ever lived in. My entire life, good and bad, was wrapped up in these walls. Something needed to change.

The screen door clattered closed behind me.

"Home," I called out to no one in particular. Mom and Dad were used to my schedule. I kept it like clockwork. Online college, visit next door, online college, sleep, repeat. Unlike the usual teen, I was easy to track and never left home. It wasn't always like that. Before.

"In the kitchen, honey," Mom called.

I ignored the clutter in the living room, which normally drove me crazy, and strolled toward the inviting smells of dinner.

"Got the mail." I plopped the stack on the white Corian countertop.

"How was your day?" Dad asked from the kitchen table, his work papers spread out in an unorganized mess.

"Nothing new." I closed my eyes and inhaled the familiar aroma of fresh crawdads. Comfort.

Turning toward Dad, I did a quick inventory. He looked tired, too old for his fifty-four years.

His full head of gray hair accentuated his silver-blue eyes, and the laugh lines had turned to frown and worry lines. That was all my fault.

"How's Ada Lynn?" Mom busied herself with adjusting her red and white checkered apron. Her hand reached up to smooth her brown hair, now streaked with white. I didn't remember when, exactly, but Mom had long since stopped her fun routines—getting manicures, massages, and having her hair highlighted. Also, my fault. Now she just tied it in a bun and ignored the nicks in her fingernails. Shadows of my past lingered everywhere I looked.

"Same."

Awkward conversations had immersed our home in grief, held us hostage after the year we never spoke about. The year I stopped living and began to merely survive.

I wandered over to the steaming pot on the stove. The letter in my back pocket crinkled as I bent over and eyed the potatoes, mushrooms, and corn. My mind whirled with thoughts of the acceptance letter for college in Washington. I'd sent the application on an impulse. On one of the rare days I believed I could be strong enough to have a life again. Louisiana was in my blood. If I left, I'd miss everything about it. Most of all, I'd miss Ada Lynn.

Although my mind was ready, I wasn't sure I could force my body out the front door and past the dirty white picket fence. Could my feet carry me past Ada Lynn's house and to the bus stop? My shoulders tensed at the mere idea. Like I did with everything else that terrified me, I pushed the thought away and busied myself with other things.

After dinner, I washed the dishes, my mind floating back and forth between the letter from the university and my parents. Even though it had been five years since my world had shattered, the blackness still lingered. A permanent ink stain on my soul.

My mother's sudden gasp broke the silence.

"What?" I asked, drying off the last plate, placing it in the cabinet above my head, and turning toward her.

"Nothing," she replied. I didn't miss her attempt to cover up a piece of paper with her hands.

Dad's expression grew grim as he stared at her.

My spine tingled, and tension claimed the air between us.

"Are you sure?"

"I'm fine," Mom snapped.

"I have a paper to write," I mumbled and tossed the towel on the counter, walking away.

My bare feet padded lightly across the smooth wood floors as I rounded the corner and stopped, waiting for their conversation to begin.

"It's from her," Mom said in a hushed tone.

"Again?" Dad asked.

"Shh, keep your voice down. Gemma can't know."

"Even if she did, we've prayed about this, and it isn't God's will for her," Dad stated.

"Kyle don't start with me. Where was God when all of this happened?"

My skin hummed with anxiety. Who were they talking about? My brows knitted together as I wondered what I'd missed in the stack of mail today. I'd been so distracted by the acceptance letter I hadn't bothered to look through the rest.

I fiddled nervously with the hem of my T-shirt and waited.

"My God," Dad whispered, his voice breaking.

My chest tightened when I heard my mother quietly crying. I walked back toward my room. It would only be a matter of time before they fell asleep, and I could try to find out what had rattled them so much.

I slipped into my bed and stared at the white walls of my room. Stark white. Nothing. Blank. It's what my life had become. However, something deep inside me stirred, ready to be free.

THE HUM of the cicadas filled the otherwise quiet night. I kicked off the sheet, sat up, and placed my bare feet on the floor. Mom and Dad had gone to bed hours ago, but I'd waited. Sometimes Dad woke up and raided the kitchen for a late-night snack, and I didn't want to get caught rummaging around in his office. It'd been off-limits since I was a little kid. I never bothered to ask why, nor did I care, so I stayed out. Until tonight. I'd missed something important in the mail. Important and disturbing enough to make Mom cry and Dad snap at her.

I tiptoed down the hallway and peered over my shoulder while I slowly opened the door to his office. The hinges creaked, and I stopped abruptly. After a moment, when I was sure I'd not woken them, I slipped into the room and closed the door behind me. I flipped on the lamp sitting on his spacious, cherry wood desk. The tick of the wall clock seemed overtly loud in the stillness. I expelled a long sigh as my gaze traveled around the room, taking in as many details as possible. I wiped my sweaty palms on my sleep shorts and willed myself toward his desk.

Tugging on the middle drawer, I frowned as it opened. It was empty. My confusion grew as my hands traveled down each side, opening all of the drawers, but there was nothing of any significance. Only a few blank pages of paper and a pen. Uncertainty tugged at me as I chewed on my bottom lip.

My pulse quickened as my thoughts returned to my parent's conversation earlier in the evening. I was desperate to find out what they'd been talking about. The corner of an envelope sticking out from under the large desk calendar caught my attention, and I grabbed it. My eyes drifted across my mother's name and our address, written in a graceful script. The return address indicated the letter was from Washington. Seattle, Washington. Anxiety pulled and tugged at my insides. Neither of my parents had ever mentioned any friends or relatives from there.

For the second time in one day, I unfolded a thin white sheet of paper. My forehead creased as a picture fluttered to the floor. I picked the photo up, peeked at the image, and read the back, my mouth gaping open. Cold fingers of fear wrapped themselves around my neck, and I sank into Dad's office chair. How long had the letters been coming? More importantly, how long had my parents hidden this big secret from me?

Dazed, my focus scanned the room. Several boxes were stacked in the corner, hidden in the shadows of darkness. I stood and made my way to them. Each one was marked "Office." Curious, I attempted to open the one located on the top, but it was taped shut. Damn. I wondered if there more letters inside. Logically, the items from his desk were packed, but I didn't understand why.

After reading the note for the third time, I knew that no matter what had happened, it was time to leave. I shoved the contents into the envelope, folding it small enough that I could hide it in the palm of my hand if Mom or Dad caught me walking to my bedroom.

Within moments, I was tucked safely in my bed again. My brain refused to shut off. I had some planning to do.

33

CHAPTER 2

When you have no life, you have even fewer items to pack. My belongings were minimal and consisted of clothes that likely wouldn't be appropriate for Washington's weather, along with my toiletries, laptop, and iPhone. Although I only bounced between my house and Ada Lynn's next door, my parents had bought me a cell phone. Honestly, it was a comfort, and I used some of the apps to stay connected with the outside world. Google really was a girl's best friend, and I *had* to have music. When I was in a full-blown panic attack, it was the only thing that calmed me. With my phone, I'd never had to worry about not having something to listen to.

Preparing to leave hadn't been difficult, and as far as I could tell, I hadn't raised any suspicions. I'd cleaned the house and taken care of my own laundry for a long time now, which helped to conceal my plan. It was finding a duffel bag or suitcase neither Mom nor Dad would miss that had been a challenge. Dad traveled for work sometimes, but Mom was typically home unless she ran a quick errand, which made sneaking around almost impossible. On beautiful days like today, however, she'd garden, and it had allowed me time to search the closets without gaining unwanted attention.

Even though I was nineteen, I was well aware leaving without telling my parents would scare the shit out of them. It certainly wasn't my intention, but my father believed it was God's will for me to continue to live here where I was safe. I'd already hidden behind his beliefs for far too long. I also knew he would stop me from walking out of the house if he caught wind of my plans.

Unfortunately, it meant Ada Lynn was my partner in crime, and my parents would be left with nothing but a note. I was a shitty person. However, I'd learned the hard way that some decisions must be based on survival, not Dad's religious beliefs. I had to decide my past would no longer hold me hostage. Refusing to allow it to have power over me and finally doing something about it were two different things. So until my ass was on the bus and too far away to turn back, my pep talks were just a load of crap.

I tucked the duffel bag in my closet and slipped out the kitchen door into the backyard. Mom's floppy, flowered hat bobbed up and down as she dug in the dirt with her spade. For whatever reason, she loved her hats, and for a change it was in my favor. I'd packed the least offensive two I'd found in the utility room and carefully arranged the remaining ones so she wouldn't notice the missing few for a while.

"How's the garden?" I approached her.

"Better this year," she responded without stopping.

"The flowers look nice. You did a great job. You've always had a green thumb."

Her hand paused mid-dig, and she glanced up at me. "Why the sudden interest?"

"No reason. It just looks nice." I fidgeted for a moment, feeling guilty for withholding my plans from her.

Her eyes narrowed, and her mouth curved into a small smile. "Thank you. It's good therapy. Would you like to join me?"

Hesitation tugged at me for a moment while I pondered the invitation. I had no idea when I would come home, so I needed to spend the time with her.

"Sure, I can help for a bit. Don't forget I'll be at Ada Lynn's for dinner tonight."

"Oh, that's right. Thanks for reminding me," she said, handing me another spade. "Grab one of my hats from the laundry room. You'll need it to protect your fair skin from the sun."

I nodded and hurried inside, taking the first one I saw. Other than Ada Lynn's porch, I'd not spent a lot of time outside and never in the direct sunlight. Placing it on my head, I adjusted it and grimaced. Regardless of how much I despised it, I'd have to get used to them.

I tucked my hair into the hat and peered into the small square mirror hanging on the wall next to the door, my shoulders slumping forward with the look. It was awful.

Thankfully, my hair had lightened to a coppery red as I'd grown older. According to Mom, the only red hair in my family was my Aunt Kim's dark red pubes, and for years I had agonized over the fact it had somehow ended up on my head. When it had lightened, it brought much-needed mental relief. Especially when Aunt Kim visited, and I could focus on spending time with her instead of staring at her in horror.

The same year my life turned upside down, Aunt Kim passed away suddenly from an aneurysm. One moment she was talking to a coworker, and the next she had dropped dead on her office floor.

Mom had never fully recovered from the sudden loss. Maybe if I left, she would be able to move on as the constant reminder of everything she'd lost would no longer stare her in the face.

I made my way outside, inhaled the sunshine and summer air, and knelt next to Mom. For the next hour and a half, we dug in the dirt and tended the garden in silence. And for the first time since I could remember, it wasn't awkward. It was peaceful. I'd tuck this memory in my heart and cherish it forever.

ADA LYNN'S kitchen was barely large enough to hold the two of us. She sat at the small, four-person square table in the middle of the floor while I worked at the stove, boiling noodles, and making her favorite spaghetti sauce. I'd opted to use her countertop toaster for the garlic bread.

Even with the air conditioning, it was too hot to turn on the oven.

"You ready for your trip?" Ada Lynn asked while I strained the noodles.

"No." My chest tightened as I placed the plate in front of her, pulled out a chair, and joined her.

"It won't be easy but remember I'm only a phone call away."

"What if I can't do it?" I stared down at my spaghetti.

"You can do it. And when you're so scared you think you're going to puke your dinner up, you just remember if you come back, you'll never leave again. So don't. Don't come home for a long spell. Nothing ever changes 'round here anyway. So what in God's name would you miss?"

"You," I muttered, twirling noodles around my fork.

Ada Lynn's hand found mine and squeezed.

"Promise me you'll make it. There's only one thing I want to see before I pass on, Gemma. I want to see you moving forward and living your best life. Do it for an old woman. Email me updates and pictures of your beautiful smile and new friends. I'm not great on the computer, but you taught me how to email, so it will work out just fine."

My attention dropped to my plate and traveled to her again. Her eyes glistened, and tears welled in mine.

"Promise," she said sternly.

"Promise." My pulse raced with my word. She knew I'd do everything in my power to keep it.

"All right then, let's eat. I've got a bit of a treat for us." A mischievous grin spread across her face as we returned to our food for a minute.

"You know where to find my extra car key. Just lock it up and park it at the bus station. They don't know it yet, but your mom and dad will help me pick it up and bring it home. Hell, I hope it starts." She chuckled, spinning noodles around her fork.

My brows shot up. "Why wouldn't it? I started it last week and let it run."

"I know. However, the car is almost as old as I am."

"No, it's not." I rolled my eyes at her and we smiled. "I'm going to miss you most of all," I said, my heart sinking into the pit of my stomach.

"Likewise. And I'm not going anywhere yet, so I expect weekly updates."

"You got it."

We finished dinner, and Ada Lynn directed me to her top cabinet.

"Right there, the jar. Get it down and grab some glasses."

When I rejoined her at the table, I twisted the lid and opened the glass container, peeking inside. If I'd been able to see my own expression, I probably would have broken into a fit of giggles.

"What the hell?" I peered at her from the corner of my eye.

"Moonshine," she chuckled, taking it from me and pouring a little into each glass.

"Ada Lynn, are you trying to get me drunk on my last night in Louisiana?"

"You'll be fine, just don't drink it fast. Besides, I'm not giving you much."

I raised the glass and sniffed it. My focus cut over to her as she took a drink and shuddered.

"Go on now." She waved at me to hurry up.

"It's a good thing I'm leaving. You're a bad influence," I teased. Sucking in a quick breath, I took a drink. My cheeks flamed with the heat rising up my neck and ears as the alcohol burned down my throat and into my stomach. Seconds later, a fireball worked its way up, depleting my mouth of any air and moisture. A coughing fit followed, and Ada Lynn patted me on the back.

"Pretty tasty, huh?" She wiggled her eyebrows at me.

"Are you trying to kill me?" I sputtered between coughs.

"Of course not. Just a bit of toughening up before you leave. Try it again, it'll go down easier."

I took a small sip and grimaced, but I didn't hack up a lung this time. Progress.

Another hour ticked by as we talked, and she sipped her alcohol. Two tastes had been enough, and I was positive they would last me a lifetime.

The mood grew solemn, and before I realized it, it was time for me to head to the house. There were only four more hours before I slipped out the front door and drove away. Nausea swirled in the pit of my stomach, my dinner and drink churning.

"It's time," I said.

My chair scraped across the linoleum floor as I scooted away from the table, watching her while she leaned against it and stood slowly. I wrapped my arm around her and embraced her.

"Thank you," I muttered.

"Good luck." Her warm breath tickled my ear while her arms wrapped around me. I bent down and hugged her for a full minute. Letting her go had never been an option before. Tears streamed down my cheeks and into her thin hair.

"I love you, Ada Lynn. Thank you for believing in me," I whispered.

"Love you too, my blue-eyed girl. You call when you reach the school, so I don't worry myself to death."

"Yes, ma'am." We released each other, and she squeezed my hand in hers.

"Go, now. I'll talk to you soon."

Our tears flowed freely as I stepped away, grief seeping deep into my bones. I wiped my cheeks with the back of my hand, gave her a small wave, and left her standing in the kitchen—alone.

The door closed behind me, and I made sure it was locked before I sat down in my chair on her porch and quietly sobbed into my hands. How in the world would I get through each day without Ada Lynn? I hated the thought of leaving her behind. Stepping onto that bus tomorrow was going to be the hardest thing I'd ever done.

In the corner of my mind, Ada Lynn's voice broke through my whirlwind of emotions, reminding me I'd made her a promise. After everything she'd given me, I owed it to her to do the best I could—give her what she wanted before she left this world.

My body shuddered with one last cry, and I sucked in a deep breath. Standing, I squared my shoulders, walked off her porch, and to my house. The distinct aroma of Dad's cigars filled the night air. Shit, he was outside on the porch. I hoped he hadn't heard me crying. At least the darkness would hide my tear-stained cheeks.

"Hey, Gemma. How was dinner?" he asked as I hopped up the front porch steps and sat in the cedar porch swing next to him.

"It was fun. I made her favorite, spaghetti."

"That was sweet of you." He puffed on his cigar, the embers glowing brightly.

An image of the packed-up boxes flashed across my mind, and I toyed with the idea of asking him about his empty desk. It was probably no big deal. He had most likely just cleaned things out, donating the items or something. Besides, if he knew I'd been in there, he'd realize I had the letter. He couldn't know I actually did have the letter until I was far from home in another state.

"How's work?"

Dad paused for a minute. "I haven't wanted to say anything, but I lost my job."

"What? I thought you were working last night at the table." I gasped. "Why didn't you tell me?"

"Because I didn't want you to worry. You have enough on your plate, and I want you to focus on college."

The packed boxes, now I understood.

"What are you going to do?"

"Well, I'll search for another job. I have a few leads already. Most companies have an operations position or something similar, so it'll be fine. I suspect the interviews will come in next week. I mean it. Don't worry. We've got money put away in case of an emergency, so we're fine."

"Really? You're not just saying it?" I asked, chewing on my thumbnail, attempting to contain my nerves. A small part of me hoped this was my excuse to stay.

"No, we really are okay." He offered a sad, reassuring smile.

After mulling over what he'd said, I realized this was one more reason why it was time for me to leave. He'd supported me long enough. I needed to figure out how to take care of myself now.

"Okay. I trust if we were in trouble, you'd tell me. I'm going to try and get some sleep. Are you coming in soon?" I paused and waited for him to reply.

"In a bit. I'm going to finish my stogie, then I'll be on in. Night, honey."

I stood, leaned over, and kissed him on his forehead. "Night. Love you, Dad."

"You too. And Gemma, we're going to be fine, you have my word."

Our eyes locked briefly before I nodded and turned away to enter the house. Guilt nagged at me for not telling him I was leaving. If all went well, though, he'd find out in the morning. I hoped he'd see it as a positive thing, one less burden to carry, but he was a strong proponent for me never leaving and remaining tucked away for the rest of my life. If it were only that simple.

Mom's soft snore came from the couch when I entered the front door. My lips pursed, and I offered a silent prayer that she would wake up and go to bed. I watched as her chest rose and fell, my heart aching while I planned my next move. She deserved so much better than the hand she'd been dealt.

I crept down the hall and brushed my teeth for the last time in my bathroom. Tears blurred my vision as I rinsed my mouth and gazed in the mirror. My blue eyes were one of my best features, other than my now copper-red hair. I pulled on my ponytail holder, allowing my soft, loose curls to flow over my shoulder. Since it was red, I'd planned to hide it underneath Mom's hats while on the college campus in Spokane, Washington. Thank God she had a few plain denim choices instead of all that floral. There was no way I wanted to attract attention, and I assumed with the cold weather a lot of people wore hats. Honestly, I just wanted to keep my head down and concentrate on my degree. I would have enough to adjust to with sharing a room and people around me on a regular basis. Not to mention dealing with four actual seasons.

Ever since I'd made the decision to go to Spokane, my heart hadn't stopped trying to escape my chest.

I flipped off the bathroom light and walked toward my bedroom. Dad's deep tone carried down the hallway while he woke Mom up and guided her to their room. A sigh of relief escaped me. I was grateful I wouldn't have to try and sneak past her out the front door.

I peeked at my alarm clock. The countdown had officially started. One hour gave me enough time to pack the remaining items that would have caused my parents to raise an eyebrow. I had to be painfully quiet and make sure not to wake them, though. Unplugging my clock, I shoved it in my oversized duffel along with my bedspread and pillows. It amazed me how much I could stuff in the bag.

Dinner churned in my stomach. Saying I was

terrified was by far an understatement. I was scared shitless. But every night I stared at these walls, I died inside a little more. Whatever it took, I had to learn to live again. Not only for me, but for Mom, Dad, and Ada Lynn.

Midnight. It was finally time to leave. With shaking hands, I shoved my toiletries into the last bit of space in my bag. The sound of the zipper echoed in my stripped clean room. I hoped like hell I could lift it. It hadn't even crossed my mind until now.

I scanned the room one last time, a single tear slipping down my face. Inhaling sharply, I grabbed my duffel, stepped out, and closed the door gently behind me. My eyes adjusted to the darkness as I glanced toward my parents' room. Thankfully, all was still. I crept my way through the hall and into the kitchen, grabbing the container of food I'd prepared with snacks for the trip. If Ada Lynn hadn't mentioned it, I would have forgotten to take any food at all.

My hand trembled as I placed the note on the kitchen table. They would see it after they poured their mugs full of coffee and sat down in the morning. My throat tightened. If I didn't leave now, I'd find myself within the safe walls of my room again, unpacking instead of walking toward a new life.

"Goodbye," I whispered.

A few minutes later, I tossed my duffel bag on the front seat of Ada Lynn's car and slipped inside.

"Please start, please start," I muttered, inserting the key and giving the ignition a turn. To my relief, the car roared to life.

Light shattered the darkness when Mrs. Brownstein's porch light flicked to life. I squinted against the brightness and remained still as she peered through her living room window in my direction. Clutching the curtains around her neck, she looked like a disembodied ghost keeping watch over the neighborhood.

With newfound courage, I shifted into reverse and backed the fifteen-year-old Cadillac out of Ada Lynn's driveway. Tears rolled down my cheeks as I slipped it into drive, my foot pressing the accelerator. I wiped at the tears, cleared my vision, turned on the radio, and drove the ten minutes to the bus station. As I focused on the dashboard clock, I realized I would barely make it. Panic shot through me.

I couldn't miss my bus! I pushed harder on the

accelerator, exceeding the speed limit. Thankfully it was late, and the streets were empty.

I let out a shaky breath when I saw I'd made it in time—the bus was still at the station.

After parking the car, I quickly grabbed my bag, jumped out, and hit the lock button on the key fob. I would mail it to Ada Lynn as planned once I got settled.

"Hey!" I yelled when I saw the bus doors folding shut. "Wait! No!"

My feet pounded the pavement, but the weight of the duffel slamming into my legs was too much.

Everything moved in slow motion, right before I smacked into the asphalt face first. Pain shot through my body, but the cry which escaped my lungs was caused by the sight of the bus slowly moving forward.

I shoved myself up and waved my arm in the air, hoping someone would notice me and stop the driver.

"No! Stop!" I yelled with one last effort.

Nothing. The bus didn't slow. Instead, it continued to move forward cautiously into another lane.

A cry lodged in my throat. Shit, I'd failed. I

couldn't even run away right. My head hung down with defeat.

"Hey! Come on now. Hurry up!"

"What?" My head jerked up. "I'm coming! I'm coming!" I picked up my duffel and ran, the bag banging against my shins with every step. He'd stopped. Thank God, someone had seen me. A stitch started in my side, and my breathing came in ragged bursts from the weight of my cargo.

I stumbled up the stairs of the bus and dug into my pocket for my ticket.

"Thank you," I said, gasping for air.

"Be glad someone back there saw ya." He nodded as he closed the doors, the bus jerking forward. I staggered and limped my way to an empty seat in the middle. My body collapsed in a spot next to the window. I'd made it. Covering my mouth, I choked more tears back. I took a shaky breath and attempted to regain my composure as the parking lot faded into the distance, and we pulled out onto the main road, heading toward the interstate. It was going to be a long trip, but at least I'd taken the first step.

34

CHAPTER 3

Three and a half days later, I stepped onto the college campus. Spokane was a far cry from Louisiana. The sidewalks bustled with busy students, lugging boxes and suitcases toward the dorms. Parents followed behind them and picked up their dropped items. A knot twisted in my stomach. I'd never seen so many people in my life.

Dazed, I struggled to take it all in, trying not to let my nerves get the better of me. My mouth hung open slightly as I absorbed the vast buildings, the architecture, towering trees, and green grass. Everything was green here. In Louisiana, burnt and brown were the colors from July through October. Nothing compared to what was in front of me, breathtaking.

"Are you lost?" a voice asked beside me, causing me to jump. "It's okay. It can be a little overwhelming in the beginning. You'll get used to everything."

"Not sure if I will, but thanks for the vote of confidence," I muttered, and peered at the woman next to me who had obviously noticed my newbie sensibilities. My gaze connected with soft brown eyes and a gentle smile. Thankfully, my nerves calmed a bit.

"Do you have your information? I can help you." She held her hand out toward me. "I'm Savannah, by the way. I'm a senior. I volunteer to help the newbies for the first few weeks."

"Oh, yeah," I said, digging in my front pocket with my free hand. A moment later, I presented her with a piece of paper.

"Gemma," I said as I adjusted my floppy denim hat and the green-tinted glasses I'd put on before the city bus dropped me off. As much as I disliked them, they were now a permanent part of my daily attire. "Guess I'm searching for my dorm."

"Okay. Are you new to Spokane? Your accent is pretty thick," Savannah asked, her brow arching. She handed my information to me and waited for my response.

"Yeah. I just got off the Greyhound from Louisiana."

"You must be exhausted," she said, her eyes wide. "And I know exactly where your dorm is. I'm heading that way. It's close, but with your bag it would be a tough walk. I'm happy to give you a ride."

I kicked at the sidewalk with my well-worn tennis shoe. My stomach knotted. I was always wary of a stranger offering me a ride.

"It's okay, maybe if you can point me in the right direction?"

"Sure, I can. Oh, wait, I've got a better idea. I know someone else who has already moved in. Let me call her, and she can meet us here and take you. You'll like her. She's...well, she's Mackenzie," Savannah said, laughing.

I fisted my hands to stop them from shaking and forced myself to calm down. Remain aware and assess the situation, I reminded myself. The most important thing for me to remember was to listen to my instincts. My attention dropped to the sidewalk, and I inhaled slowly in order to contain the blooming fear inside me.

"Mac? Hey, I've met someone new who just

arrived from Louisiana, and she's utterly lost. She's in the same dorm you are in. Can you meet us at the student center? Yeah? You're the best, thanks." Savannah disconnected the call and peered at me.

"She said she's up the road and on her way. So how did you end up here in Washington?" she asked, shoving her cell in the back pocket of her jeans.

"It was far away from Louisiana, and they offered me a full ride," I mumbled. I figured it was close enough to the truth.

"Well, welcome to the Inland Pacific Northwest," she said, her smile lighting up her face.

"Thanks." I shuffled from one foot to the other while she continued the small talk.

A car horn blared behind me, and I yelped. My hand covered my mouth as my cheeks heated.

"Mac! You scared the shit out of her," Savannah scolded.

I turned around, and a dark-haired girl with braided pigtails rolled down the passenger's window.

"Sorry!" She waved for me to come closer. "I'm Mac. Grab your stuff, I'm headed to the dorm now."

My eyebrow arched as I shot Savannah a look.

"She's harmless, I promise," Savannah said, patting me on the shoulder, reassuring me.

"Um, oh okay. Thanks for your help." Against my better judgment, I snatched up my bag and hefted it into her back seat. A moment later, I settled into the passenger's side and buckled up.

"Packed kinda light, didn't you?" Mackenzie asked as she checked her mirrors and slowly merged onto the street.

"I don't have much. Don't need it."

"That's great you keep it simple and welcome to Spokane! What's your name? Savannah didn't say, and I'm pretty sure it would be super rude not to ask you, right?"

"Gemma," I said, slipping in my name when she took a breath.

"I love it," she replied. "You don't hear that name very often. I think it's beautiful, and I bet you do, too."

Flinching from her volume, I felt terrible for her roomie if she always spoke this loudly. Chiding myself, I remembered she was being kind and driving me to the dorm.

"This is my sophomore year, and I'm getting my degree in art. That's how I met Savannah. She's majoring in art, too. What are you majoring in?"

"Criminal justice," I replied, surprised I could sneak an answer in between her incessant chatter.

I cracked my window for some fresh air. Between her energy and voice volume, the car had started closing in on me. The last few days on a cramped bus had left me eager to stretch my legs, but instead I sat in a small car with a very loud, petite human being.

"Do you like music?" she asked, her finger darting out to hit the power button. The speakers blared with heavy metal.

Oh my God. What had I done? I cringed, reminded myself to breathe, and prayed the ride would be short. Suddenly, an overwhelming pang of sadness tugged at my heart while my mind wandered to Ada Lynn. We should be on her porch right now, watching the last golden rays of the sun dip behind the hills. I hoped like hell my parents weren't angry at her for helping me leave.

"Here we are." Mackenzie pulled up to the dorm, breaking through my thoughts. I assessed the red brick building and shrank into my seat. It was huge. Surely my entire hometown could fit inside it.

"Thank you!" I yelled over the tunes while I opened the car door and grabbed my bag. With a deep sigh, I headed up the walkway. I reached into my pocket for my dorm room information and continued through the front doors. Families were filing into the building and milling around the huge lobby, bumping into me as we all made our way toward the elevator. Since I'd been sitting so much over the last several days, I opted for the stairs even with my heavy bag. Two flights and a mile-long hallway later, I stopped in front of my door. Room number 250. I sucked in a quick breath, along with some courage, and opened it.

The room was small with hardwood floors, white walls, two twin beds, and built-in dresser drawers. One side was already unpacked. Well, I wouldn't really call it unpacked. Instead, a pile of unfolded clothes and items were scattered all over one of the beds. If she kept her sloppiness to her side, I could learn to deal with it.

I dropped my bag in front of the closet and peered inside. It was small, but it would work.

My ears perked up as a group of girls ran screaming through the hallway. Startled, I jumped backward, landing on my ass. Giggles continued, so I assumed everything was okay and no one was hurt. Grateful no one had seen me overreact, I pushed myself off the floor and made quick work of unpacking.

When my stomach growled, I realized I needed to find a cafeteria somewhere to get some decent food. I'd subsisted on junk food for days— vending machine snacks and the occasional burger. And I was hungry.

First, I wanted to call Ada Lynn. I had also promised her some pictures. After I snapped a few of me in my new room, I emailed them to her.

My lips pursed as my phone screen flashed with seven missed calls, each one from my father. I'd been so wrapped up in my escape to Washington I'd refused to deal with the worry and stress I'd surely put them through. Refusing to dwell on it, I deleted the messages without listening to them. I knew him well enough to predict what they'd say.

This isn't God's will, young lady. You should be ashamed of yourself; God is.

My fingers tapped my screen, and seconds later, the line on the other end rang.

"Hello?"

"Ada Lynn, it's me."

"Gemma, you arrived in Washington safely?"

"Yes, ma'am. How are you? How are Mom and Dad?"

Ada Lynn's chuckle filled the phone. "Pissed. We didn't expect anything different, though did we?"

I smiled sadly, and my heart ached to be with her.

"I'm so proud of you. You made it. Now just don't come back," she said.

"I'm going to do my best. This place is insane, and it's huge."

"It sounds like it's a big change, but you can do this, Gemma. You call me a few times a day if you need to. I'll remind you of the big ol' nothin' you're missing down here. Your parents may be a bit upset, but they are okay, so don't use them as an excuse either."

She knew me well, and I had to keep in mind this move was good for my parents, too. They'd spent too much time hovering over me and had given up their own lives in the process.

"Yes, ma'am. How pissed are they?"

"Oh, really mad. Your dad took to yelling at me, and I had to put him in his place real fast. However, your mom, she was shocked, but she's also proud of you. Give them some time, and they'll come on around. You take care of yourself and remember your promise."

"I will."

"Love you, now you go on and find some new friends and call me tomorrow."

"Love you, too."

A tear snuck down my cheek as I ended the call and shoved my phone in my back pocket. My stomach reminded me it was past time to eat. I adjusted my hat and tinted glasses in the mirror. No one here knew I didn't need them to see. They just hid my face, and I could observe people without them seeing my eyes very well. The unique color of my hair and eyes had always brought unwelcome attention. I never used to mind it, then everything changed.

Somewhat content with my appearance, I headed out of the dorm in search of food. One of the most significant challenges I would have to deal with was the noise level. Since I'd attended an online college, I'd never dealt with other students, or the usual college antics—high-pitched girl screams, loud guys making asses of themselves around cute girls, so on and so forth.

On the bus ride to Washington, I'd memorized the essential places on campus and how to reach them from my dorm, so I had a general idea of where to find my meals.

My worn, second-hand Converses smacked against the pavement of the sidewalk as I took my time walking, cautiously taking inventory of my surroundings. Frowning, I pushed my glasses up my nose. I'd definitely have to get adjusted to them. The tint was enough to hide the color of my blue irises, but it was also more challenging to see things.

I had a few hours before the sunset, which allowed me to explore the campus a bit.

I peered at the trees, the numerous brightly colored flower baskets, and the lush, green grass. The smell of the freshly cut and manicured lawns tickled my nose. It was beautiful, and I never wanted to lose this moment of seeing everything for the first time. Nothing was skewed or ruined. It was brand new and alive.

Loud laughter jarred me from my thoughts. My head jerked toward a group of five rowdy guys approaching me.

"Hey baby, where'd you come from?" a tall, athletic dark-haired guy asked me.

Completely ignoring him, I continued to walk.

"Hey, trailer trash, I'm talking to you. Where'd you buy those clothes?"

The guys hooted and punched each other on the shoulder like the insult had been the best they'd ever heard. I ignored them and moved forward. It wasn't anything I hadn't been around before. And for whatever reason, I didn't care what they thought of my clothes.

"Why don't you take them off and let me see what you've got underneath? Maybe some perky tits? A cute little ass? Hard to tell with your cheap, shitty clothes hanging off you like that. And your fucking hat is horrible. Did you take it off your dead grandma's head?" he asked, his volume growing louder with each word.

I kept my attention straight ahead and met his insults with silence.

"Hey, bitch. I'm talking to you."

Anger dripped from his words. Fear wrapped its cold fingers around my throat, and my hand dug into my front pocket, ready, just in case he moved forward.

"Dude, come on, leave her alone. If she wants to wear a potato sack, let her," another guy piped up.

Even though I tried not to, my focus turned toward them as they grew closer. My pulse double-timed while they broke out into hysterics. One of them stared, hands shoved in his jeans' pockets, but he remained quiet. His eyes were trained on me as I walked around them, ignoring the comments and heckling. If I fed into it, they'd win.

Fortunately, the asshole had a short attention span, and moments later, when they found some other girl to harass, I ducked around the corner of a building. Knots formed in my stomach, my legs gave out from under me, and I fell to the ground on my hands and knees. Trembling and unable to support myself, I dropped flat on my tummy and breathed in the aroma of the grass and dirt. Black dots danced across my vision, and I clawed at the lush green blades, willing my heart rate to slow down.

When I felt steady enough to stand, I pushed myself off the ground. Still shaky, I placed the palm of my hand against the building, the coolness of the shaded stone comforting me. I cautiously peeked around the corner and thanked God the guys were nowhere to be seen. My eyes scanned the structure for a name and immediate relief spread through me. It was the library. I made a mad dash for the front door and pulled my phone out of my pocket, unwrapping the headphones as I hurried through the lobby.

The second I stepped inside, the familiar scent of books greeted me, and I inhaled deeply. Shoving my earbuds in my ears, I tapped my Spotify app and went to my playlist. The librarian eyed me curiously, but I ignored her and went in search of the fiction section.

After finding one of my favorite books, I plopped into a chair at a small table in the back corner and placed my forehead on the wooden surface. This was better. Books and music, minimal people around me.

Flipping the novel open, I scanned the first page and willed my body to calm. My foot began to tap to Citizen Shade's "Funk War," the music cloaking me in safety. He could sing anything and make it sound good. I'd never heard another voice like his either.

Although I'd read it multiple times, I slipped into another world as soon as I started reading *The Hunger Games*. Ten pages in, a hand snuck across the table and tapped a finger on the surface next to my book. My hand automatically jerked away, and my head snapped up at the intrusion. Folding my hands in my lap, I scowled at the guy who had settled into the chair diagonally from me. His expression was serious as he flipped his shoulder-length wavy brown hair over his shoulder. He ran a hand over his closely trimmed facial hair as his angular jaw tightened, and he motioned for me to remove my earbuds.

"What?" I asked, my tone clipped. He wasn't invited. This was my table.

"Are you okay?" His bright blue eyes flashed with concern.

My eyebrows knitted together in confusion.

"Sure," I replied. If he got his answer, maybe he would leave.

"No, I'm serious, are you okay? You almost passed out behind the library. I was there working on something," he said in a hushed tone.

My mouth gaped slightly. He'd seen me have a massive panic attack? I'd not seen anyone, but my knees had hit the ground so fast I hadn't had time to look.

"I'm fine." Heat spread across my neck and ears, giving away my emotions.

The weight of his gaze was unnerving as we stared at each other silently. Although my stomach churned, I refused to let him know how much he had unsettled me. My chin tilted up in defiance. I wasn't his problem, and I certainly didn't want him hanging around.

"There are plenty of other tables," I offered and nodded toward them.

"Okay. I just wanted to make sure you were all right. I didn't mean to bother you." He pushed his chair back and stood. "Nice glasses," he mumbled before walking away.

Was he being a smart-ass, or was he serious? Maybe the hat was awful, but the glasses weren't.

My attention lingered on him as he made his way to another table. I'd not seen a hot guy since middle school, and even though I fought it, I was intrigued. His jeans hugged his lean legs and tight ass, his white T-shirt stretched across his muscular shoulders. However, his hair was the feature that grabbed me the most. It was perfection, and I had to resist the urge to reach out and touch it.

He probably got that a lot, girls wanting to touch his hair. The color of his eyes was almost as striking. In reality, though, none of this mattered. I still wondered what he wanted from me. I'd have to be careful moving forward; no more panic attacks in front of other people.

He glanced in my direction as he sat down at another table not far away. I inserted my earbuds again and attempted to settle down into my story. However, my brain wasn't having it. After another ten minutes of struggling to focus, I gave up. I closed the book, stood, and shelved it. My finger tapped my phone screen, and I turned off my music.

I strolled by him on my way out, and his gaze followed me as I passed. Pushing through the front doors of the building, I struggled to control my breathing. Attempting to clamp down my anxiety, I leaned against the brick of the building. I hated my need to question the motives of every person who talked to me. The only people I'd had direct contact within the last five years were my parents and Ada Lynn. I was so out of practice! Inwardly I cringed as hope of ever trusting anyone again dwindled away.

My stomach growled to remind me I still needed to eat something, and I headed toward the student center. I had enough time to grab a bite and head to the dorm before it got dark.

AN HOUR LATER, with a full stomach, I pushed open the dorm room door and entered my new home. A girl sat on the floor in a lotus position with her back to me, a tan knit cap covering her head.

"Almost finished," she said so softly I struggled to hear her.

I waited patiently for her to turn around so that I could meet my new roomie.

A young woman hopped up from the floor, whirled around, and ran toward me at full speed, knocking me against the door. Her arms wrapped around me as she hugged me.

"Roomie! I'm so excited we already met."

Dear God, it was Mackenzie. I was the poor roommate who would have to put up with her loud-speaking volume and heavy metal music.

She released me, and my heart sank. She looked at me with such a hopeful expression, I immediately felt conflicted. I needed quiet and calm. She was anything but that. However, she'd been so nice and welcoming to me.

"I'm so glad it's you. I'm so sorry, if I'd known I would have walked you up here myself instead of just kicking you out of the car," she said in a rush of excitement.

Struggling to regain some sense of composure, I offered her an awkward smile. Thank God she couldn't see my expression behind my glasses. I closed my mouth and tried to form any word in the English language. I was stumped about how to handle the moment, though.

Mackenzie grabbed my hand and tugged me across the room, talking nonstop. She adjusted her blue jean overalls and turned toward me, speaking so fast I had a difficult time keeping up with her.

"Wow, you all dress a lot differently in Louisiana," she said, eyeing me. "What do people say? Never judge a book by its cover. But I totally do, so I'm apologizing now. I bet you'll be the best roomie I've ever had and we'll be best friends. And since you don't have your family here, you can share mine. I'll introduce you to everyone I know, and we can go to any classes together we might share..." Her hazel eyes widened as she jumped up and down. "Oh my God, I'm so excited."

"I can tell," I said, managing to fit in a word.

"Call me Mac, all my friends do." She flitted to her side of the room as I walked backward toward my bed and sat down in utter shock. I'd never met someone that moved and talked so fast. Was everyone here like this, or was it just Mac?

"Oh, one thing you should know about me. I'm ADHD. Do you know what that is? Attention Deficit Hyperactivity Disorder. Yup, it's me. And I tried the meds, and oh my God, they made me feel like shit, so I stopped taking them. If I can focus enough to pass my classes, I don't ever want to take them again. My mom wants me to, though. She doesn't know how to handle my ball of energy. And, like, I don't sleep a lot so do you have some noise-canceling headphones you can use in case I'm watching TV or something? Maybe an eye mask, so the light doesn't keep you awake? And enough about me, tell me all about you. I want to know everything."

Once again, my mouth gaped open as she tossed her clothes to one side and plopped down on her bed, propped herself against the wall, and honored me with a toothy grin.

"I've never met anyone who talked this much," I said.

"Oh, you'll get used to me. At least I hope you will. And sometimes, like when you need to study or whatever you *have* to tell me to shut up. If I know I'm dancing on your last nerve, I so get it, and it's not what I mean to do. Seriously, I want you to like me, I mean we're roomies for an entire year." Her voice hit a high pitch, causing me to wince. "Okay, I mean it, tell me about Louisiana, and I'll shut the hell up."

Anything to get this girl to hush sounded like a good idea to me.

The second my mouth opened to speak, she charged in again.

"Do you eat crawdads? Ew, are they disgusting? I've only read about Louisiana, I've never been to the south, but your accent is fucking amazing." She paused briefly. "Wait, oh gosh, I didn't just offend you with the F-bomb, did I? I won't use it again, if it's not okay, it's one of my most favorite words, like ever."

I held my hand up to her. "Give me a minute."

"Oh sure, you're probably super tired from the trip, and—."

"Stop," I said. "Please."

Mac frowned as she slumped forward. "Sorry," she muttered.

Oddly enough, a few moments of silence permeated the room. Something I sorely missed already.

"I only arrived a few hours ago, and I'm overwhelmed and exhausted. Yes, I have earphones, but I won't use an eye mask, or I'll have nightmares and don't want to scare you. I can tell you about Louisiana one question at a time. It's the only place I've ever lived until today, so some patience would be appreciated. I'm also adjusting to a two-hour time change. It's part of the reason I wanted to arrive a few days early, to settle in and catch my breath. And my favorite thing in the world is peace and quiet."

"Oh boy. I've scared you already. Sorry."

This time Mac stopped talking instead of running over at the mouth. Maybe I could train her with positive behavior reinforcement.

"Do you like chocolate?" I asked, working out the scenario in my head. Good behavior deserved chocolate.

"Yes, however, the sugar makes me hyper, so it's a rare treat."

Inwardly, I groaned. The last thing I wanted to do was make her more hyper. I seriously doubted it was even possible.

My pulse raced as I realized Mac would be the one person who saw me without glasses and my hat. I forced myself to remove them and tossed them on the desk next to my bed.

"Shit, why do you wear a hat? You have the most beautiful hair I've ever seen, even with it all messy," she said, hopping off her bed and peering at me, her face mere inches from mine. I flinched when her hand shot out and touched my hair. "And your eyes, you're beautiful. Why would you hide?"

I raised my hand again to stop her.

"Keep this to yourself, Mac, and we will be

best friends. Obviously, we're living together, and I have to shower and stuff, but you won't see me in public without my glasses and hat. Don't ask questions, it's just the way it is. Do you understand me? Don't tell anyone, don't mention what I look like without them or anything else. It stays in this room. Are we clear?" My words carried a steel tone, and she straightened.

"Best friends if I keep your secret?" She twirled her braid around her forefinger, waiting for my answer.

To continue Gemma and Hendrix's story in Love & Ruin, click here or click here for the boxset.

***

Important note!

I realize there are a lot of unanswered questions about Hendrix and his past. As you read Love & Ruin, you'll learn more about Kendra, Franklin, Mac, Janice, Cade, and John as Hendrix falls in love with the girl in the glasses. When Gemma finally reveals who she is, I hope you love her as much as I do. Women with a past like hers are never weak. Overcoming trauma takes more guts than anyone can imagine except those of us that have walked that path. I speak from my own experience. At one time I identified as a victim, then a survivor. I no longer identify as either. I refused to allow my past to define me as I rebuilt my life one strong brick at a time.

I say this with so much love in my heart: To every woman who has survived trauma and rebuilt her life, Gemma's story is for you. We are truly stronger together.

OTHER BOOKS BY
INTERNATIONAL BESTSELLING
J.A. OWENBY

Bestselling New Adult Romance

The Love & Ruin Series

Love & Ruin

Love & Deception

Love & Redemption

Love & Consequences, a standalone novel

Love & Corruption, a standalone novel

Love & Revelations, a novella

Love & Seduction, a standalone novel

Love & Vengeance, a standalone novel

Love & Retaliation

The Wicked Intentions Series

Dark Intentions

Fractured Intentions

The Torn Series, inspired by True Events

Fading into Her, a prequel novella

Torn

Captured

Freed

Standalone Novels

Where I'll Find You

Love & Sins

J.A. OWENBY

Edited by: Hot Tree

Cover Art by: iheartcoverdesigns

Photographer: Furious Fotog

First Edition

ISBN-13: 978-1-949414-38-7

Gain access to previews of J.A. Owenby's novels before they're released and to take part in exclusive giveaways. https://www.authorjaowenby.com/

A NOTE FROM THE AUTHOR:

Dear Readers,

If you have experienced sexual assault or physical abuse, there is free, confidential help. Please visit:

Website: https://www.rainn.org/

Phone: 800-656-4673

This book may contain sensitive material for some readers. Gemma and Hendrix's story is considered a dark romance with language, sex, and violence.

ACKNOWLEDGMENTS

To my husband, you are my forever. Thank you for being my biggest supporter.

ABOUT THE AUTHOR

ABOUT THE AUTHOR

International bestselling author J.A. Owenby grew up in a small backwoods town in Arkansas where she learned how to swear like a sailor and spot water moccasins skimming across the lake.

She finally ditched the south and headed to Oregon. The first winter there, she was literally blown away a few times by ninety mile an hour winds and storms that rolled in off the ocean.

Eventually, she longed for quiet and headed up to snowier pastures. She now resides in Washington state with her hot nerdy husband and cat, Chloe (who frequently encourages her to drink). She spends her days coming up with ways to torture characters in a way that either makes you want to throw your book down a flight of stairs or sob hysterically into a pillow.

J.A. Owenby writes new adult and romantic thriller novels. Her books ooze with emotion, angst, and twists that will leave you breathless.

Having battled her own demons, she's not afraid to tackle the secrets women are forced to hide. After all, the road to love is paved in the dark.

Her friends describe her as delightfully twisted. She loves fan mail and wine. Please send her all the wine.

You can follow the progress of her upcoming novel on Facebook at Author J.A. Owenby and on Twitter @jaowenby.

Sign up for J.A. Owenby's Newsletter:
BookHip.com/CTZMWZ
Like J.A. Owenby's Facebook:
https://www.facebook.com/JAOwenby
J.A. Owenby's One Page At A Time reader group:
https://www.facebook.com/
groups/JAOwenby